Oct 2018

DREAMWORKS
TROLLHUNTERS
TALES OF ARCADIA
FROM GUILLERMO DEL TORO

THE WAY OF THE WIZARD

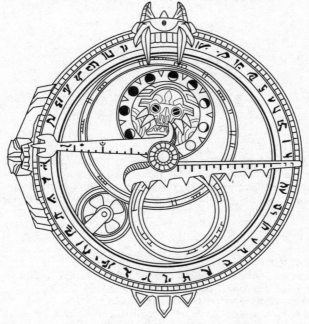

Written by Richard Ashley Hamilton
Based on characters from DreamWorks Tales of Arcadia series

Simon Spotlight
New York   London   Toronto   Sydney   New Delhi

SIMON SPOTLIGHT
An imprint of Simon & Schuster Children's Publishing Division
1230 Avenue of the Americas, New York, New York 10020
This Simon Spotlight hardcover edition October 2018
DreamWorks Trollhunters © 2019 DreamWorks Animation L.L.C. All Rights Reserved. All rights reserved, including the right of reproduction in whole or in part in any form. SIMON SPOTLIGHT and colophon are registered trademarks of Simon & Schuster, Inc. For information about special discounts for bulk purchases, please contact Simon & Schuster Special Sales at 1-866-506-1949 or business@simonandschuster.com.
Designed by Nick Sciacca
Manufactured in the United States of America 0818 FFG
10 9 8 7 6 5 4 3 2 1
ISBN 978-1-5344-2865-2 (hc)
ISBN 978-1-5344-2864-5 (pbk)
ISBN 978-1-5344-2866-9 (eBook)

In all his many centuries of life, Kanjigar had never known such happiness. Yes, he had felt thrilled when Rundle, son of Kilfred, father of Vendel, admitted Kanjigar into the select order of Troll scholars. And, of course, Kanjigar had been overjoyed the day he wed his bride, Ballustra. This elation only doubled later, when Kanjigar removed a chip of his own living stone, fit it against one of Ballustra's, and embedded the matching pieces in a small crystal. But even that moment paled against the swelling Kanjigar now felt in his heart.

After watching that crystal grow and glow for three decades—the average length of time for Troll development—Kanjigar and Ballustra finally heard the first, faint crack of the Birthstone. They rushed to the splintering crystal just in time to see a little blue foot kick through its opaque surface. Warm, pink light shone from within as Kanjigar broke away more shards of Birthstone and Ballustra breathed, "Husband . . . we have a son."

Kanjigar knelt before the little Troll staring back at him. Their eyes were the same. Yet Kanjigar recognized tiny versions of Ballustra's horns protruding from the newborn's head. Ballustra took their baby into her arms, nuzzled his face, and asked, "What shall we call him?"

"Draal," said Kanjigar, recalling his favorite Troll scholar.

Young Draal seemed to enjoy the name too. He smiled and gurgled while Ballustra handed him to her husband. And as a father holding his son for the first time, Kanjigar now experienced the most overwhelming sense of pride. Of peace. Of completion.

This was the greatest happiness Kanjigar had ever known.

"Look at his arms," Ballustra marveled. "He'll make a fine Monger Troll indeed!"

Kanjigar's smile faltered. He had just been inspecting Draal's eight perfect fingers. The thought of those chubby hands holding weapons—which Monger Trolls like Ballustra made exclusively— seemed inconceivable. Kanjigar pushed the image from his mind, ignoring the imaginary war drums he had started to hear . . . only to realize they weren't quite so imaginary.

"That's a Gumm-Gumm combat march," Ballustra said, also hearing the rhythmic beat echo into their cave. "It's getting louder. Closer."

"Closer than you might think!" cried a familiar voice.

Kanjigar instinctively held Draal tighter as the Galadrigal brothers, Blinkous and Dictatious, barged into his cave, their dozen eyes bulging in terror. But when he saw the baby Troll, Blinkous clasped his four hands and added, "By Gorgus, your child is born! What a blessed occasion on such an accursed day!"

Dictatious squinted six beady eyes at Draal and said, "Is he *supposed* to look this odd?"

Ballustra moved to strike Dictatious. But Kanjigar held her back and said, "Dictatious, Blinky, you honor us as our son's first visitors. Yet what makes this day so 'accursed'? What brings those drums of war to our very threshold?"

Calming himself, Blinky said, "The Gumm-Gumms have invaded Trollmarket. Our Trollhunter, Gogun the Gentle, does his best to keep them at bay, but their numbers are legion!"

"And you've come here to *hide*?" asked Ballustra, her contempt apparent.

"No, not to hide. Only to inform Kanjigar that the Gumm-Gumms are sacking the scholars' library as we speak," Blinky said.

"But also to hide," Dictatious added hastily.

"Then it seems we've been blessed with *two more* babies on this day," said Ballustra.

She crossed to her worktable and picked up an iron crossbow loaded with crystalline arrows. As Ballustra adjusted its bowstring, Kanjigar placed a hand on her spiked shoulder.

"Wife, do not do this," said Kanjigar. "Do not go out there."

But Ballustra said, "It is my skill to make arms and my duty to take them up in battle. I am a Monger."

"You are also a mother," Kanjigar replied. "Right now, our son needs you more than our Trollmarket. To leave our cave is to welcome death."

"Ah, but death needs no welcome," growled a darker voice. "It goes wherever it pleases."

Kanjigar felt Draal squirm in his arms, frightened by this new presence. Ballustra whirled around and aimed her weapon at the entrance to their home. Through the crossbow's sights, she saw an enormous Gumm-Gumm filling the entirety of the doorway, his hulking body threaded with veins of pale blue energy, his single eye burning bright.

"Gunmar the Black!" Blinky exclaimed.

"Begone, Gumm-Gumm," Kanjigar said bitterly. "We hold no quarrel with you."

"Yet you hold something else of interest," Gunmar snarled, black bile dripping from his jowls. "For I seek to add to our mighty ranks . . . with a recruitment drive."

Kanjigar realized with horror that Gunmar now looked directly at young Draal, as if sizing him for a miniature set of Gumm-Gumm armor. The monstrous Troll stepped deeper into the cave and said, "Enlist your whelp in my army. Or he dies on the same day he was born."

Ballustra tightened her finger around the crossbow's trigger while Kanjigar tightened his grip around their son. Gunmar moved closer, only for Blinky to defiantly block his path and say, "Now hear this, foul one! None of us will *ever* serve you! Isn't that right, brother?"

"Well . . ." Dictatious demurred from his hiding place behind Ballustra.

"You speak as though you have a choice," Gunmar said, knocking aside Blinky.

The towering Gumm-Gumm's right claw flexed, summoning pale strands of energy from his veins and molding them into the Decimaar Blade. Gunmar pointed his sword in Draal's direction and growled, "Give me your offspring—NOW. With luck, he may survive the rigors of my training and become as fine a killer as my own heir."

Kanjigar looked beyond Gunmar to see a second Gumm-Gumm darken his doorstep. This one was smaller, but his red eyes bore the same merciless glare. Still recovering on the floor, Blinky looked up and gasped, "Bular!"

Gunmar and Bular filled the cave with matching howls, making baby Draal cry. In response, Ballustra fired her arrow directly into Gunmar's chest. The Gumm-Gumm general grunted in pain, then grunted again as he yanked the crystal bolt from his hide. Bular pulled twin swords from the scabbards across his back and stalked toward Kanjigar and Draal.

Kanjigar's first thought was to shield his son from the oncoming beast. But the young Troll slipped out of his hands before he could even react. Bewildered, Kanjigar watched his son's plump face screw into an angry pout and rocky spikes pop out of his back, just like Ballustra's. Young Draal then grabbed his toes, tucked his little, naked body into a ball, and rolled headlong at Bular with incredible speed.

Caught off guard by the bizarre sight, Bular could only watch as the Troll tyke gave a tiny roar and crashed into him like a living boulder. The impact toppled Bular, sending his swords spinning in opposite directions. Kanjigar and the Galadrigals stood in stunned silence, until Blinky said, "I believe this means Draal's first word was 'RRRAAH!'"

Kanjigar reclaimed his son and looked over to Ballustra, who now fought off Gunmar's Decimaar Blade with a matching pair of battle staves. Their weapons smashed and sparked against each other, until a grating, out-of-tune horn blew in the distance.

"It's the Gumm-Gumms—they're sounding their retreat!" Dictatious said.

"Gogun must have turned the tides!" cheered Blinky.

Bular retrieved his swords, while Gunmar readied the Decimaar Blade for a final slash. But the horn blared again, far more urgently this time, followed by a stampede of hundreds of Gumm-Gumms away from Glastonbury Tor Trollmarket. Gunmar kept his one eye fixed on the family of three, even as he vanished his Decimaar Blade in a cloud of brimstone.

"You *will* serve me," Gunmar said to the infant Draal. "One day . . ."

Ballustra and Kanjigar tensed their bodies, ready for another violent attack. But Gunmar gave a low, decisive snort to Bular. The two Gumm-Gumms backed out of the cave just as quickly as they had trespassed into it.

Once the last blast of the horn faded in the distance, signaling a full withdrawal, Ballustra tossed aside the staves and took Draal back into her arms. She cradled him so close to her own body, she could feel his small heart beat against her own. Kanjigar looked at what was left of their meager belongings. He saw the broken crib and toys he'd built in anticipation of Draal's arrival, now crushed from when Bular had been bowled into them.

"You have our thanks, Kanjigar, for offering us safe haven," said Blinky. "And you, Ballustra, for defending us so vigorously."

"It's Draal who deserves your thanks, not I," said Ballustra, hoisting her boy in the air like a hero. "Not an hour out of his Birthstone and already felling grown Gumm-Gumms!"

"Hear, hear!" Dictatious called. "To Draal!"

"To Draal!" echoed Blinky.

Kanjigar was the only one to not repeat the words. For the sublime happiness he'd enjoyed upon his son's birth was now replaced by the sharp pang of a new paternal feeling—worry.

"To Draal the Deadly," said Ballustra. "The greatest warrior Trollkind shall ever know!"

CHAPTER 1
REST IN PIECES

Twelve hundred years after his birth, Draal the Deadly was dead.

Jim Lake Jr. dropped to his knees. He stared wordlessly at the lifeless stone body of the Troll, the bodyguard, the *friend* who'd fallen to his death so that Jim might live. It had taken the young human Trollhunter a while to descend into the geode pit, to scale the massive white crystals studding its walls. The fact that Jim's clothes and shoes were waterlogged—the result of his recent escape from a submerged catacomb—hadn't helped during the arduous, slippery climb. But now that he'd reached the bottom and seen Draal's remains illuminated in the crystals' harsh glare, Jim didn't know what to do next.

When Jim and Draal had first met, it was as enemies. Draal believed the Amulet should have chosen *him*, not some fleshbag, after leaving its previous champion—Draal's own father, Kanjigar. And so Draal challenged Jim to trial by combat, only for the newly minted Trollhunter to best his blue, spiked opponent. Even more surprising, though, was the way Jim broke with Troll custom afterward and spared Draal's life. As a means of repayment, the humbled son of Kanjigar made an oath to guard the Trollhunter, his mother, and their home.

And Draal had indeed kept his promise, protecting Jim's loved ones and training the Trollhunter in swordsmanship. The loyal Troll had even sacrificed his own right arm to thwart one of Gunmar's earlier attempts to escape the Darklands. Now, Jim understood, Draal had sacrificed the rest of his body in service of his beloved Trollhunter— just as the Gumm-Gumm king had eventually succeeded in returning to the surface world. But to lose Draal, with Gunmar still alive and free, seemed so pointless to Jim . . . so unfair . . . so unreal . . .

For a while, all Jim heard was the soft pat of teardrops against his knees, adding to the denim's dampness. Then, from a respectful distance, a voice softly said, "Master Jim?"

The Trollhunter stood, quickly wiping his eyes with the back of his sleeve. He saw his six-eyed Troll mentor, Blinky, reach the base of the pit, followed by the rest of his soaking-wet friends—Claire Nuñez, Toby Domzalski, and AAARRRGGHH!!!

Claire hugged Jim, the streak in her hair all the whiter under the crystals' light. She said, "We got worried when you didn't come back up. We thought maybe you and Angor Rot—"

Angor Rot.

Jim's mind flooded with hatred for the assassin who'd killed Draal. Team Trollhunters had long believed Angor Rot dead, only to discover he was back and working for Gunmar. And Jim had been so focused on stopping Gunmar earlier, he hadn't noticed Angor Rot stalking behind him, his dagger laced with lethal Creeper's Sun poison. But Draal noticed. Draal put his body between Jim and the dagger. Draal turned to stone and fell to his doom. Not Angor Rot. Not Gunmar. Not Jim.

"Not possible," Jim muttered through clenched teeth.

Claire looked up at Jim, her wide eyes searching his. He looked away and said, "Angor Rot's gone. He must've escaped this pit and the mountain above us somehow. I . . . I'm sorry I made you worry, Claire. All of you. I guess I just wanted to be alone for a bit. . . ."

Toby joined Jim and Claire, making it a group hug, and said, "No disrespect, Jimbo, but when someone says they want to be alone, that's usually the time *not* to leave them alone."

The warm reunion ended when they heard a panicked yell, followed by a tremendous racket. Seconds later, an old, bearded figure landed on the floor in front of them. The latecomer dusted off his emerald armor, adjusted his skullcap, and said, "Greetings, everyone. What'd I miss? Besides that third crystal step, that is?"

"Dude, are you *sure* you're Merlin?" asked Toby. "I know you just took us on a magical tour of Troll history, but I always pictured someone a lot less . . ."

"Accident prone?" suggested Blinky.

"Clumsy?" added AAARRRGGHH!!!

"Slapsticky McClownpants?" offered Claire.

"All the above," finished Toby.

"Ah yes, kick the wizard when he's down, is it?" muttered Merlin. "As if all your legs would work properly after a *thousand-year* slumber? Why, if you hadn't let my Staff of Avalon fall into Gunmar's claws, I'd use it to teach the lot of you some manners—starting with the chatty one who smells of toffee."

"It's nougat, actually," Toby corrected cheerfully.

"To-may-toe, toe-mah-toe," said Merlin. "And tell me something. Is *everyone* in this era always this dour? I've seen happier faces at a funeral—"

"Merlin, please!" hissed Blinky.

The six-eyed Troll nodded toward Jim, who had returned to Draal's side. Blinky leaned closer to the wizard and, in a low voice, added, "Perhaps you might impart some wise words of comfort to our Trollhunter?"

"Hmm? Oh yes," said Merlin absentmindedly. "Yes, I suppose I could say something to bolster the boy's resolve."

Jim and the others watched as the wizard

stood over Draal and held out his hands with great authority, as if about to cast a powerful spell. Merlin cleared his throat and closed his eyes.

"Here lies a warrior true, his words were few, and mostly said as a battle cry," he began.

Jim sighed heavily, remembering Draal's legendary temper and aversion to small talk.

"It's such a shame, er, with Gumm-Gumms to blame, that Draal's gone to that big Hero's Forge in the sky," Merlin finished in a rush, clearly making up that last part on the fly.

Startled by the eulogy's abrupt conclusion, every single member of Team Trollhunters glared at the wizard. But none more so that Jim.

"Not! Helping!" Blinky snapped at Merlin.

Claire arched an angry eyebrow, and one didn't have to be a sorcerer to understand what the look meant: *Not cool.* She shook her head, turned toward her boyfriend, and said, "Don't listen to him, Ji—"

Claire cut off. She saw Draal's stilled form, but no Jim keeping vigil over it. Team Trollhunters then heard the squeak of Jim's wet sneakers as he climbed out of the geode pit.

"I'd better talk to him," said Toby, hitching up

his pants in preparation of the long ascent.

"No talk, Wingman," AAARRRGGHH!!! said. "Jim want quiet. AAARRRGGHH!!! go."

Toby and AAARRRGGHH!!! shared a silent fist bump before the musclebound Krubera Troll bounded up the white crystals after Jim. Blinky pinched the space between his many eyes in frustration and said, "How could a wizard be so clueless when it comes to human feelings?"

"I, Merlin, am *clueless*?!" Merlin repeated with umbrage.

"Aha! You admitted it! No take-backs!" said Toby, flashing a braces-filled smile.

"'Take-backs'?" Merlin said in confusion. "What are 'take-backs'? Some breed of Goblin or Gnome or some such?"

As Toby explained "take-backs" to the fascinated wizard, Claire turned to Blinky and said, "This is bad. I've never seen Jim so upset, and Gunmar and Angor Rot have a major head start on us."

"Agreed," Blinky said, rubbing his chin in thought. "Our considerable loss here at Merlin's Tomb has brought Gunmar one step closer to the prophesied Eternal Night. I suggest we table our grief for the moment and return to Arcadia Oaks posthaste."

"You don't have to tell me twice, Blink," said Claire. "As soon as we get out of this magic-free mountain, I can shadow-jump us to—"

"Ahem," interrupted Merlin. "There won't be any 'shadow-jumping.'"

"Because there's an even faster way back? Like a super wizard gyre?" asked Toby. "Word of warning, though. I don't do so well on gyres. Especially after Taco Tuesdays."

"No," Merlin said flatly. "No gyres, no Shadow Staffs, no travel spells. And no tacos."

Blinky did some quick mental math and said, "Merlin, the distance between your mountain and Arcadia is more than seven thousand miles! How, exactly, do you propose we return home?"

"It's simple, really," Merlin said with a shrug. "We'll walk."

CHAPTER 2
TWO TROLLS WALK INTO A CAVE . . .

"What?! That's crazy talk!" roared a River Troll.

He slammed his fist into the hot oil bath—one of many natural pools of crude that had formed in the underground cave—splashing the second River Troll beside him.

"Shmorkrarg speak true," said the second, the large boulder atop his head adding extra emphasis. "Shmorkrarg saw Garden Trolls sneak into River Troll camp, plant their ugly seeds."

"Those mossy meddlers!" said the first River Troll. "If I ever get ahold of them, I'll kick 'em so hard in the gronk-nuks, they'll—"

The River Troll's voice trailed off as large bubbles appeared on the oil bath's surface. He pinched his nose and said, "Aw, Shmorkrarg!"

"That not Shmorkrarg!" said Shmorkrarg. "Shmorkrarg not raised in barn like Helheeti!"

Before the other River Troll could say *yeah, right,* he saw the oil around them instantly turn bright red. Startled by the blossoming color change, both River Trolls leaped out of the bath and hollered, "It's cursed!"

Shmorkrarg and his friend then heard laughter. They squinted in the dim light provided by the cave's gemstones, until the first River Troll pointed ahead and shouted, "Look!"

On the other side of the cave, two Garden Trolls slapped their knees, the leafy branches sprouting from their crowns shaking as they continued to laugh.

"More Garden Troll mischief!" said Shmorkrarg.

He and his friend marched over to the Garden Trolls, who wiped their eyes and deposited the moisture onto the lichens they'd been growing in this cave. The first River Troll said, "What'd you peat pushers do to our oil bath?"

"Easy, now, river rubbish," said one of the Garden Trolls with a hint of warning.

In retaliation, the first River Troll stomped on

the lichen patch. Shmorkrarg shoved the Garden Trolls and said, "You pollute Shmorkrarg's oil bath!"

"That wasn't us!" yelled the first Garden Troll.

"But we sure thought it was funny!" said the second as he shoved Shmorkrarg back.

The River and Garden Trolls tackled one another. They traded kicks and punches on the lichen bed, both sides spitting out insults as they fought. Shmorkrarg was about to use his boulder to head-butt one of the Garden Trolls when he heard a strange sound.

Fwip.

Half a second later, Shmorkrarg felt a metal rope wrap around his torso, pinning his arms to his sides. He lost his balance and fell over, landing with a thud on the trampled lichens. The remaining Trolls gaped in surprise before—

Fwip. Fwip. Fwip.

Three more coils cinched around their bodies too. Heavy crystal bolas at the ropes' ends spun into place, forming unbreakable knots. Dazzled by the spinning crystals, the Trolls tipped over and joined Shmorkrarg. They all writhed on the cave floor, trying to break free, but it was futile. Shmorkrarg looked over his shoulder and saw a hooded Troll approach, twirling more of those crystal bolas.

"The longstanding feud between the River and Garden tribes has lain dormant for centuries," said the Troll in the hood. "But if you bickering fools seek to end that fragile truce, don't do it with mere *fists*."

The cloaked Troll stopped spinning the crystal bolas and pulled out a sharp knife. All four trapped Trolls took one look at the gemstone blade and squirmed even more urgently.

"He crazy!" shrieked Shmorkrarg.

The River and Garden Trolls all cried out in terror as the knife sliced at them—only to see that the blade had slashed their ropes, not their bodies.

"Return to your respective camps," said the hooded Troll, before handing the gem blade to the River Trolls. "And keep that as an example of my craftsmanship."

Now freed, the River and Garden Trolls scrambled away to their home caverns. The Troll under the hood trudged toward the oil bath, now faded to murky pink, with bits of trash floating on its surface. Scooping a hand into the oil, the mysterious Troll retrieved a few foil wrappers plus several dropper bottles filled with some manner of red dye. A circular white tablet fell out of one of the wrappers and plopped into the bath, making the oil around it fizz with more bubbles.

The hooded Troll sniffed the foreign items, then muttered a single word: "Humans."

Had that Troll not been wearing a hood, Porgon the Trickster might have been discovered in his hiding place. Lurking behind a large rock several feet away, Porgon struggled to stifle his giggles. The Trickster Troll just couldn't help it. He'd seen two Trolls walk into a cave, then take a relaxing soak in the oil bath. And when the Garden Trolls appeared soon thereafter, an idea for a prank mushroomed in Porgon's twisted mind. He looked down at the splotches of red dye and fizzy white powder on his hexing hand and experienced another fit of giggles. Because Porgon knew the *real* fun was just about to start. . . .

CHAPTER 3
SEVEN THOUSAND MILES TO HOME

Jim stormed out of Merlin's Tomb, squeezing the Amulet so hard his knuckles were as white as the snow now billowing around him. Icy winds tempered the intense warmth radiating from his flushed face and neck. Looking out from the tomb's entrance, the Trollhunter saw Europe's famed Ardennes Mountains spread before him. From the way their peaks sloped, it appeared as if the entire range had turned its impassive back to Jim, unconcerned with whatever paltry emotion he felt right now. To combat the cold, Jim held out his Amulet. It ticked again now that Jim had crossed the painted symbol forbidding outside magic in Merlin's lair.

"For the doom of Gunmar, Eclipse is mine to command!"

In an ebony swirl of otherworldly energy, the Eclipse armor manifested from the ether. The Trollhunter's black-and-red figure stood in stark contrast to the pristine snow, like some demon that had gotten incredibly lost on the way back to whatever dark place it called home. He trembled inside the armor, not from the frigid gales, but from the anger that boiled within him. Jim retracted the faceplate from his horned helmet and screamed as loud as he could.

The anguished cry only stopped once Jim's lungs had run out of oxygen. Spent, he slumped onto the ground. Jim heard his howl echo against the mountains before the winds overpowered it with their own scream.

"Feel better?" grumbled a gravelly voice.

"Not at all," Jim said as AAARRRGGHH!!! emerged behind him.

The gentle Troll shut his eyes in understanding and sat next to Jim on the frostbitten turf. They remained there for a while, not talking, just watching the horizon start to lighten.

"Sun come up soon," said AAARRRGGHH!!! "Always does."

"Then we'd better find shade," Jim said. "Or being near me will turn *you* to stone too."

"Wouldn't be first time," AAARRRGGHH!!! joked.

Jim heaved with another sigh and said, "We got so lucky, AAARRRGGHH!!! To have you come back to life like that. And I guess I got extra lucky in a weird way. I was so busy trying to survive in the Darklands back then, I didn't even have a chance to mourn the two weeks you were gone. But that luck . . . it finally ran out. I mean, I've had friends come and go before. Heck, even my dad up and left one day. But this . . . this is different."

AAARRRGGHH!!! turned his round, sympathetic eyes toward Jim. Twin trails of frozen tears glistened on the Trollhunter's face.

"I've never had anyone I've known—that I've loved—die before," finished Jim.

The Krubera Troll wrapped his arm around Jim. Now feeling very tired all of a sudden, Jim leaned against his friend and said, "There's so much I didn't get to ask him, AAARRRGGHH!!! So many things he still had to teach me about wielding a sword. I never even got to thank him for the way he protected my—oh no . . ."

Jim abruptly twisted the Amulet off his breast-plate, vanishing the Eclipse Armor. AAARRRGGHH!!! watched him pull out his cell and dial the first contact in his favorites list.

"C'mon, c'mon," Jim said as the phone started to ring, knowing this long-distance call would deplete what was left of his low battery—and rack up one heck of a roaming fee.

Dr. Barbara Lake couldn't answer her phone fast enough. She raced out of the kitchen, where she'd been overcooking snacks for the many individuals crowded into her house.

"Everyone, quiet!" Barbara shouted, reaching her cell on the coffee table. "It's them!"

The numerous houseguests—Ophelia and Javier Nuñez, Nana Domzalski, Dictatious, NotEnrique, Gnome Chompsky, and Walter Strickler—went silent, awaiting any news about their children and friends. On the third ring, Barbara answered, turned on the speakerphone, and said, "Jim! Jim, we got your last text! That's great news about finding Merlin and—"

"Mom," Jim said.

Barbara had never heard her son's voice sound so grave. At least, she thought she hadn't. It had only been one day since Barbara figured out Jim was the Trollhunter—for the second time, that is. Jim and his Troll friends had erased the truth from Barbara's memory to protect her. Clearly, everyone had expected this knowledge to send the overprotective mother over the edge. But Barbara welcomed it, surprising all but herself. It was as if things had gone back to the way they were before Jim became the Trollhunter, before secrets had come between them.

"What is it, kiddo?" asked Barbara, masking her worry. "Are you hurt?"

"No, it . . . it's not me," Jim finally confessed. "It's Draal. Angor Rot killed him."

Ophelia, Javier, and Nana traded confused looks, having never met the Troll that once resided in Barbara's basement. But Strickler, Dictatious, NotEnrique, and Chompsky gasped. They had known Draal well, having fought alongside—and sometimes against—him.

"The son of Kanjigar . . . *slain*?" said Strickler, aghast.

"That's 'orrible," added an unusually serious NotEnrique. "Draal may've been a one-armed party pooper, but he was *our* one-armed party pooper."

Barbara turned off the speaker, held the cell to her ear, and said, "Oh, Jim, I am so sorry."

"Me too, Mom," he said back, his voice cracking on that last syllable. "He really liked you. Even if he never could pronounce your name."

"When are you coming home?" asked Barbara. "I know it probably seems silly, but a hug from your mother might help. I know it'd make me feel a lot bett—"

The line went dead. Jim checked his phone and saw the empty battery icon before the screen went blank too. He jammed the cell into his pocket and said, "Well, that's just perfect."

AAARRRGGHH!!! watched Jim don the Eclipse Armor once again, then heard the rest of Team Trollhunters as they exited Merlin's Tomb and felt the bracing mountain air. Toby shivered and said, "Okay, how about just a tiny teleport to Brussels, then we catch a flight—business class, preferably—to Newark, with a connection to—"

"No! Magic!" said the wizard adamantly. "As it

stands, I can scarcely conjure little more than *parlor tricks* without my staff. Besides, I've been napping for close to one thousand years. I could use the exercise."

Before Toby could respond, the wizard proceeded down the mountain, whistling contentedly. Blinky threw his four arms into the air and exclaimed, "Great Gorgus, this Merlin is a madman!"

"And he's locked my Shadow Staff!" griped Claire. "I can't jump us anywhere!"

She extended her staff and concentrated with all her might. It barely generated an itty-bitty black hole between its tines, far too small to admit any of them.

"The old coot wants us to hoof it all the way back to Main Street!" Toby told Jim.

"No," said the Trollhunter.

Claire took his armored hand into her own and said, "Jim, I know you're upset. We all are. But, honestly, I can't see any other way for us to get off this mountain."

"That's not what I meant," answered Jim, heading back into the tomb. "We'll go the way the wizard wants us to. But we're not leaving empty-handed. . . ."

CHAPTER 4
FAMILY FEUD

"So it begins," said the Elder Garden Troll, shaking his broken branches in dismay. "And so it ends."

The two Garden Trolls before him—the same duo that had escaped the hooded Troll—exchanged a grim expression, as did the hundreds of other Garden Trolls gathered in their great, grassy cavern. Stooping over, the Elder plucked a flower that was equal parts plant and crystal, and said, "Long have we Garden Trolls clashed with the River tribe."

He crunched the delicate blossom between his fingers. As its glittering petals fell, the Elder said, "But this latest provocation—this defilement of our sacred lichen patch—signals the end of our so-called truce . . . and the beginning of all-out war!"

A hush spread through the crowd, its members

turning to one another in shock at their leader's words. The shock soon gave way to tribal pride, though. Each Garden Troll stood a little taller and grunted, as if girding themselves for battle.

Seeing the broken flower sparkling at his feet made the Elder think back thousands of years ago, to his childhood and the start of the troubles with the River Trolls. The same crystal flowers had grown in the Garden Trolls' lands then, and the Elder took special care in cultivating them. One day he'd been merrily tending his garden when a boulder struck him in the head and snapped his crown of branches. In a daze, he saw a lone River Troll pointing and laughing at him from the cliff that loomed over the flower beds.

"Now you look like River Troll!" he had said.

Thus, the seeds of revenge had been planted in the humiliated heart of the Elder—and the hearts of *all* Garden Trolls.

"Re-venge! Re-venge! Re-venge!" chanted the River Trolls.

Their Ruler suspected this would happen. When she heard how two Garden Trolls sullied their sacred oil bath, the River Troll Ruler knew the truce had been broken. Just as she knew that convening every River Troll in the shallows of their underground lake would end in a call to arms. But even the wise Ruler had not suspected just how eager to fight her tribe had become.

As the River Trolls churned the waters with their belligerent stomping, the Ruler studied its currents. See the tides shift reminded her of another time, thousands of years ago, when she had just become acting Ruler.

The River Trolls had known a simple life then, their days as placid as the subterranean streams in which they dwelled. But one day those waters stopped flowing. The Ruler traveled upstream and discovered the source of the drought: a humungous dam erected out of the same phosphorescent trees harvested by the Garden Trolls. No sooner had she walked up to inspect the glowing timbers than they began to groan, buckle, and snap. The pent-up water pressure burst the dam wide open. Out cascaded thousands of gallons, washing away the Ruler and flooding the River Trolls' aquifer, changing the flow of its streams forever.

The Ruler thought she could still feel water from that deluge clogging her ear canals now. But the throbbing in her head came instead from the River tribe's escalating chants for retribution. The Ruler took the gem knife, looked at the two River Trolls who brought it to her, and said, "Tell me more of this hooded Troll—and his fantastic *weapons*. . . ."

Some thought jokes were only funny the first time they heard them, not the third or fourth or even *five hundredth* time. But Porgon disagreed. No, that dam made from Garden Troll timber was just as funny to Porgon now as when he built it on a whim ages ago. So was dressing up as a River Troll and braining that flower-sniffing Elder with a boulder. *Classic!*

Porgon loved running gags, and this one had been going on for generations. But thanks to his recent mischief, the Trickster Troll knew all these centuries of setup were finally going to reach their payoff.

Because the Garden Trolls and the River Trolls were about to go to war.

CHAPTER 5
SALT IN THE WOUND

Jim tasted salt on his tongue, though his tears had dried about five miles ago. No, this briny flavor came from the very air he breathed. Merlin had led Jim and the rest of Team Trollhunters into an underground tunnel to avoid the rising sun. In turn, that tunnel gradually led them to a sheer crevasse, its craggy surface coated in fine white deposits of sodium chloride.

"I don't know if this much salt's good for your blood pressure, Merlin," Toby said as he sprinkled some on a Nougat Nummie. "I mean, for a wizard your age and all."

Normally, Jim would've laughed at his best friend's comment. Yet the Trollhunter wasn't feeling particularly lighthearted at the moment. Neither was Merlin, apparently. The wizard mockingly repeated Toby's words before climbing down the crevasse. The others soon followed in a single-file line: Blinky, Toby, Claire, Jim, AAARRRGGHH!!! . . . and Draal.

After Jim and his friends had gone back into Merlin's tomb, they climbed down the geode pit and retrieved their deceased friend. AAARRRGGHH!!! then strapped Draal's body to his own mossy back— just as he had once done with Deya the Deliverer's, when he carried her from one side of the world to the other. Team Trollhunters had to hurry to catch up with Merlin before daybreak, but the thought of Draal still being with them brought Jim some relief.

Only now, seeing Draal's unblinking eyes staring back at him hours later, he felt far from relieved. Jim looked down at the wizard scaling the cliff below him. A surge of resentment constricted his salt-parched throat even tighter.

Did he even say "thank you"? Jim wondered of the wizard. *We all risked our lives—and Draal gave his—just to wake Merlin up. But did we get even one kind word in return? No! All we've gotten are weird riddles and condescending remarks and, like, a full hour of Merlin complaining about lower-back pain! Well, we'll see how his back feels after I take my Sword of Eclipse and—*

"Jim?" he heard Claire say.

The Trollhunter blinked away his hostile thoughts and became aware of his position along the crevasse. He'd been so lost in his reverie that he had climbed past Claire and Toby and was closing in on Merlin.

"We're all in a rush to get home, Jimbo, but let's not lose our grip here—*literally*," said Toby as he indicated the abyss beneath them.

Tobes and his jokes, Jim thought glumly. *Always with the jokes. What a surprise.*

Jim then wondered if his friend could somehow read his mind, because Toby's expression seemed to change all of a sudden. A look of sympathy replaced Toby's grin as he said, "Look, Jimbo— *Jim*. I know how hard this is. I really, really do. But when I lost my mom and dad, Nana told me—"

"No offense, Tobes, but the last thing I need to hear right now is some greeting card message from your grandmother."

Jim only realized what he'd said after the last word escaped his lips. Claire's eyes bulged. She regarded her boyfriend as she would Steve Palchuk or any other bully at their school. Toby nodded, forced a smile, and continued descending the salty crevasse. Jim remained in place, his fingers dug into the cliffside, his brain searching for the apology he so desperately needed to give, but finding none.

"He was just trying to help," Claire finally said.

I know, Jim thought, but could not say.

"I get that people process loss in their own ways," Claire resumed. "But the truth is, everyone in Team Trollhunters has already been through that process at some point."

She pointed down at Blinky, midway between Merlin and Toby on the cliff, and said, "Blinky spent half his life thinking Dictatious died at the Battle of Killahead Bridge."

Jim watched his four-armed friend skillfully climb down the crevasse as Claire added, "I even thought *my* brother was lost forever in the Darklands. Until you found Enrique and brought him back."

But Draal isn't *coming back*, thought the Trollhunter.

"We were able to get through our grief because we had the love and support of our friends, our family," said Claire. "So you can definitely work through your feelings at your own pace, Jim. But, please— don't push away your friends and your family."

With that, Claire resumed climbing down the crevasse after Toby and Blinky. Jim watched her go and felt a sudden stinging in his eyes from the salt in the air.

Yeah, he thought. *Sure. It's the salt, Lake. Keep telling yourself that.*

AAARRRGGHH!!! lumbered past Jim down the cliff, careful to keep Draal balanced over his wide, green shoulders. Realizing he was now the last in line, Jim followed after his teammates. But the deeper they went, the harder it became for the Trollhunter to tell where his black armor ended and the darkness around him began.

After a grueling stretch of silence, Jim heard the sound of feet meeting solid ground. Merlin's emerald boots stepped onto the floor of the crevasse, and he said, "There! That wasn't so bad. Now, can any of you imagine what wonders await us beyond this salt cave?"

"Is it a pepper cave?" asked Toby.

Merlin stuck out his tongue at Toby, while Claire, Blinky, and AAARRRGGHH!!! joined them at the base of the crevasse. That just left Jim, now using his Glaives to rappel down the cliff as he did during his stint in the Darklands. Between the sounds of his handheld blades picking into the salted rock, the Trollhunter heard AAARRRGGHH!!! say, "I go first."

As the gentle giant forged ahead down the pitch-black path, Blinky turned back to Toby and Claire and explained, "Being a Krubera Troll, AAARRRGGHH!!! hails from Earth's deepest caves and sees exceptionally well in the dark. Why, just stay close behind him, and our sure-footed friend will lead us on the path to safety!"

No sooner did Blinky finish than AAARRRGGHH!!! stepped on a flat, unremarkable stone. The footfall triggered a series of unseen gears, their whirs echoing in the lightless cavern around them. A set of rocky teeth sprang out of the ground and clamped down on AAARRRGGHH!!!'s ankle, holding him in place like a bear trap.

"Uh-oh," said the large Troll.

Without warning, an array of sturdy metal bars snapped into place around Merlin, Toby, Claire, Blinky, and AAARRRGGHH!!! The two Trolls rattled the oversized cage, while Merlin merely studied its construction and said, "Hmm, impressive crafts-manship . . ."

Seeing his friends in danger pulled Jim out of his self-pity and into the present. He flipped off the cliff, connected his Glaives, and threw them in one fluid motion. The interlocked blades spun across the air and sliced at the trap, but failed to leave even the tiniest mark on its welded metal bars.

"Most impressive," Merlin said again of the impenetrable cage.

Like a boomerang, the Glaives returned to Jim's awaiting hand. He separated the blades, holstered them on his thighs, and conjured the Sword of Eclipse out of thin air.

"Stand back," he said to the others, undaunted.

Team Trollhunters heeded the warning, and Jim swung his sword against the cage. He managed to break two of the bars, but the impact reverberated throughout Jim's body. It felt like he just whacked an aluminum baseball bat against a brick wall.

"W-w-what's this thing made of?" Jim asked, his teeth still rattling.

"Shake it off, Jim," Claire encouraged from the other side of the bars. "You got this."

Seeing him in action gave her a glimpse of the old, happy-go-lucky Jim to whom she had grown so accustomed. In her heart, Claire hoped that having Jim smash this cage might bring him one step closer to dealing with his mourning, to smiling again someday. But that hope faded when she and the others heard a distinct hissing noise seep from the broken bars. Blinky took a closer look and said, "The bars—they're hollow!"

Pale, yellow smoke drifted out of them, flooding into and around the cage. As the others grew woozy around him, Merlin sniffed the fumes and said, "It's some manner of foul gas!"

"First one . . . who smelt it . . . dealt it!" Toby choked before collapsing. "No . . . take-backs!"

"Tobes!" Jim hollered.

Claire fell next, followed by Blinky, AAARRRGGHH!!!, and Merlin, their unconscious bodies now heaped in the center of the gas-spewing cage. Jim shouted for them to wake up and, in doing so, accidentally inhaled the sickly yellow vapors into his own lungs. The Trollhunter's armored hands clung to the cage bars until he, too, succumbed to an over-whelming urge to sleep.

As Jim's body crumpled to the salt-crusted ground, his bleary eyes saw the approaching shape of a hooded Troll before closing for good.

CHAPTER 6
HOUSE ARREST

"What do you mean, I can't leave?" demanded Barbara Lake. "This isn't some prison! It's my home!"

She marched past Strickler and right toward her front door. But as she stopped to grab her car keys from the foyer table, he slipped past her and blocked the doorway.

"Please, Barbara, be reasonable," Strickler implored. "With Jim and the rest still in absentia, and Gunmar marshaling his forces beneath our very feet in Trollmarket, we're *all* in great danger right now. Especially the Trollhunter's mother."

The debonair schoolteacher held out his hand, as if taking it would somehow calm Barbara. She felt the many, many eyes of her other houseguests on her. Nana Domzalski, the Nuñez family, Dictatious, NotEnrique, and Chompsky all watched from the living room like spectators at some awkward sporting event. Sighing, Barbara took Strickler's hand—only to press her thumb directly into his palm. He cried out as she applied even more pressure, then used her leverage to twist Strickler's arm behind his own back.

"The Trollhunter's mother can take care of herself just fine, thank you very much," said Barbara as Strickler squirmed in her grip. "Now, I have patients to see."

"But the hospital put you on leave!" Strickler said, wincing in pain. "So you could . . . collect your thoughts."

Barbara's eyes hardened behind her glasses. She bent Strickler's arm even further behind his back and said, "Get lost, Walt. You're good at that."

With that, Barbara released Strickler and sent him crashing into the couch. Her path now cleared, she opened the door, and looked out on her front lawn—the same lawn on which Jim and Toby used to build leaf forts as little boys. Strickler pushed himself off the couch, straightened his tweed sports coat, and said, "You're right."

Hesitating at the threshold, Barbara turned and saw Strickler take a deep breath. When he spoke again, it was with a sincerity Barbara didn't think she'd ever seen in him before.

"You clearly can defend yourself," Strickler continued, then gestured to the others in Barbara's home. "But what about them? What experience do Ophelia, Javier and, er, Nana have against Stalklings, Helheetis, and the like?"

Barbara looked from Strickler to the others in her home. They all stared back at her with such wide, lost eyes, they reminded Barbara of some of her patients—of Jim, when he was too young to look after himself, let alone wield a magical suit of armor.

"No, Walt . . . *you're* right," Barbara finally said. "We're in uncharted territory here, myself included. It's best if we all stay in our homes and wait for the kids to return."

"But how do we know our homes are any more secure than yours, Barbara?" asked Ophelia Nuñez. "How do I know my kitchen isn't overrun with Gobblers?"

"Goblins, *mi amor*," corrected Javier Nuñez.

"You won't be going alone," Strickler said, turning to the nonhumans in the room. "NotEnrique, you're more than familiar with the Nuñez household from your time as an embedded spy there."

"Wait—*what*?" cried Ophelia. "That thing was living in my house?"

"It wasn't exactly a barrel o' sweat socks for me either, lady," groused NotEnrique.

Strickler ignored them and resumed laying out his strategy, saying, "NotEnrique will accompany Mr. and Mrs. Nuñez back to their home, while Gnome Chompsky and Dictatious shall keep watch over Ms. Domzalski. If any of you spot anything out of the ordinary, contact me."

Barbara watched Strickler jot down his information onto two small sticky notes. He handed them to the others as they reluctantly shuffled out of the Lake home and returned to their own. Strickler even helped Dictatious don his cloak to avoid the sunlight outside; then he shut the door after the last of them had passed through it. Locking the dead bolt, Strickler turned around to face Barbara. She cocked an eyebrow and said, "What makes you think I was joking when I told you to get lost?"

"Please, Barbara," said Strickler. "With Draal no longer around, you need backup. Let me act as your bodyguard in his stead."

Barbara laughed bitterly and said, "Walt, the whole reason Draal became my bodyguard was to protect me from *you*. In fact, the whole reason the hospital has me on leave—to 'collect my thoughts'—is also because of *you*. So get out of my house—NOW—or the only person who'll need a bodyguard around here is *you*."

Strickler spent the rest of the morning walking around Arcadia. He told himself it was to keep an eye out for trouble, to act as a one-man neighborhood watch of sorts. But as skilled as Changelings are at lying to others, they've never been too successful at deceiving themselves.

Crossing Main Street, Strickler had to admit he'd grown to love his adoptive town. It had been centuries since he'd been sent from the Darklands to infiltrate the surface world—much as NotEnrique had some months ago. In that time, the Changeling originally known as "Waltolemew Stricklander" had traveled to many locations across the globe—Berlin,

Ranthambore, even Jersey City. Yet none of those places ever felt as much like an actual home to Strickler than Arcadia Oaks. He wondered if other Changelings felt the same way—Changelings like NotEnrique, Otto Scaarbach, and . . .

"Nomura," Strickler said.

In all the recent calamity, he'd forgotten about his fellow shape-shifter who had also defected from Gunmar's side. And if Barbara refused Strickler's protection, then perhaps she might be more amenable to Nomura's. Strickler remembered that Nomura had reapplied to her old position as a curator at the Museum of Arcadia. It had been an effective cover for her human disguise once upon a time, and the job appealed to her again as she now searched for a new direction in life.

Strickler consulted his watch. If he hurried, he figured he might be able to catch Nomura at the museum before her interview. Knowing Arcadia Oaks like the back of his (sometimes green and scaly) hand, Strickler took a shortcut through the woods, leading to the dry canal. He was about to walk down the canal's steep concrete slope, when an all-too-familiar crackling sound split the air.

"Oh no," Strickler gasped.

He ducked for cover behind some overgrown weeds and watched as a Horngazel portal opened at the bottom of the canal. A hulking figure emerged from the swirling tunnel of light and rock, and stood in the shadow cast by the overhead bridge. Yes, Walter Strickler had seen many things in many places during his many years on Earth. But none of them frightened him nearly as much as the sight before him now. For Gunmar the Gold had just stepped out of Dark Trollmarket and onto the surface world.

CHAPTER 7
UNDER THE HOOD

What a nightmare, Jim thought as he woke.

The Trollhunter was grateful to leave such a miserable dream. Even though the sun had not yet risen outside his bedroom window, he was glad to be back home, safe and sound and secure in the knowledge that Draal wasn't actually—

The sound of metal scraping against rock jarred Jim back into reality—back into the cruel reality that Draal's death had been no bedtime fabrication. He blinked a few times, and his eyes adjusted to the gloom of the new cave in which he now found himself. Squinting harder, Jim saw Toby, Claire, Blinky, and AAARRRGGHH!!! also stir beside him.

They had been freed of the cage somehow, not that it mattered. Because Jim and his friends now all sported matching shackles around their wrists and ankles, the connecting metal links scraping against the rock floor. Worse still, Jim realized that he no longer wore his Eclipse Armor, nor could he find his Amulet. The suit must've sublimated into nothingness after Jim lost consciousness, after he saw that Troll in the hood. . . .

"Oh good, you're awake," said Merlin, similarly shackled at the other end of the cave. "It feels like I've waited *another* thousand years just for you to rouse and free me."

"Can't you free yourself?" said Claire groggily. "I mean, you are still a wizard, right?"

"Oh yes, the most omniscient and omnipotent of all," Merlin said without a hint of humility. *"When I have my Staff of Avalon. Which all of you lost. To our greatest enemy. Who wants to plunge our worlds into an era of never-ending darkness. Not that I'm bitter about that, or anything . . ."*

"Er, regardless of past events, it's our present predicament that now requires attention," said Blinky. "Fortunately, there's nary a restraint built that can withstand a Krubera's strength!"

AAARRRGGHH!!! concentrated, causing the runes

etched along his skin to glow green with fury. He railed with all his might . . . only for the cuffs to remain unbroken. Blinky examined his own shackles, noticing how the metal had been marbled with traces of iridescent crystal. He then licked the cuffs, his face immediately souring at the taste.

"Sapstone!" he said between spitting sounds. "A rare underground element that saps the brute strength of any Troll, even a Krubera. But only a most skilled artisan would know how to properly alloy Sapstone with base metals. Curiouser and curiouser . . ."

Getting impatient, Jim's mind drifted to his Amulet. He needed to find it. The Trollhunter closed his eyes and expanded his other senses. He felt around the cave with his mind.

Ting!

Jim's eyes snapped open and saw the blue light flashing from across the cave. The Amulet sat on a worn workbench, surrounded by assorted tools and mechanisms. Jim telepathically commanded the device to fly into his hand as it had done countless times before.

But the Amulet stayed put.

"C'mon," Jim grimaced. "C'mon, you piece of junk!"

This new delay only added to the Trollhunter's ire. Being stuck here, shackled at the bottom of some cave about as far from home as he could get, Jim just wanted to break something—starting with that stupid Amulet.

"Can't . . . reach it!" Jim said, finally giving up.

"Reach what? *That?*" asked Merlin, pointing to the Amulet. "Why didn't you say so?"

Jim and the others watched in slack-jawed disbelief as the wizard stood, casually slipped out of his wrist and ankle restrains, and retrieved the Amulet. Merlin then handed the ticking device to Jim, returned to his spot on the cave floor, and slipped back into his shackles.

"You could've gotten out of those cuffs any time you wanted?!" Jim hollered.

"Well, I wouldn't be much of a wizard if I couldn't, now would I?" said Merlin.

"Then why aren't *you* the one freeing *us* instead of the other way around?" Jim said.

"What am I supposed to do—wave a wee wand and magically rescue you from every sticky wicket you encounter in life?" asked the wizard. "I'm afraid there are some problems you must figure out for yourself, Trollhunter."

"Fine, but does this need to be one of them?" Jim snapped, shaking his shackles. "Can't you tell that all I want to do is *just go home*?"

"Yes," said Merlin. "But I can also tell that you're not *ready* to go home. Not yet."

Jim was about to fire off some snappy retort, but it caught in his throat when the wizard's words finally sank in. Merlin took this as a fine opportunity to fold his hands, use them like a pillow on the cave floor, and pretend to go to sleep. Overcome with frustration, Jim leaped to his feet and clawed at the air in Merlin's direction—at least, as far as the shackles would allow. Once he ran out of steam, Claire leaned closer to him and said, "Jim, let it go. You have the Amulet now."

"Not that it'll matter," blurted Merlin, followed by a fake snore.

Jim tuned out the wizard, gripped the Amulet in his hand, and said, "For the glory of Merlin, Daylight is mine to command!"

Blinky, AAARRRGGHH!!!, Toby, and Claire shielded

their eyes in anticipation of the light show that was sure to follow. But the Amulet did nothing. Jim tried the other incantation.

"For the doom of Gunmar, Eclipse is mine to command!"

Again, nothing.

"The Sapstone!" Blinky declared. "It must be inhibiting the Amulet's magic!"

"Nope," said Merlin, no longer feigning sleep.

Claire snapped her fingers and said, "That knockout gas from the cage! Maybe it has some lingering side effect that's blocking the Amulet!"

"Afraid not," Merlin purred, stroking his beard.

"The problem isn't with the Amulet," Toby said. "It's with Jim."

"What?" Jim said through clenched jaws.

Toby lowered his head, just as he had when Jim snapped at him on the crevasse, and said, "No offense, Jimbo, but it's like Blinky told you on day one of Trollhunting. The Amulet's tied to your emotional state. Since you're currently flooded with all kinds of different feelings right now—and who wouldn't be?—I don't think the Amulet knows how to respond."

Jim wanted to yell. Not at Toby, but at himself for missing so obvious a truth—and for making that same, hurt expression appear on his best friend's face yet again. A few feet away, Merlin slow-clapped. He nodded at Toby and said, *"Now* I see why you keep this one around."

Jim turned over the useless Amulet in his hands, hearing an odd rattle in its gears. Midway through the third flip, Jim froze. He peered deep into the Amulet's inner workings and saw the source of the rattle—Claire's yellow hair clip, which now served as the lynchpin holding together the entire Amulet. Jim looked up at Claire with sudden insight, and she immediately read what was on his mind.

"Good thing I wear so many of these," said Claire, taking another barrette from her hair.

She bent the pink hairpin and jammed it into the keyhole at the center of her cuffs. After a few seconds of fiddling, the shackles sprang open and fell to the cave floor with a thud. Jim held out his wrists and said, "Have I ever told you how much I like your hair when it's down?"

"That's sweet," said Claire as she pecked Jim on

the cheek and opened his shackles. "But I'm not the one you should be sweet-talking."

Jim followed her gaze to Toby, who now waited for his turn to be freed. He unshackled Toby, and then Blinky, and finally AAARRRGGHH!!! Jim knew he owed his best friend the apology of a lifetime, and he wasn't going to wait another second to deliver it. Knowing that there were so many things left unsaid with Draal taught Jim that there was no time like the present to make amends.

"Tobes, I—" Jim began before a long shadow loomed across him.

Now released from the Sapstone fetters that bound them, Team Trollhunters saw the hooded Troll blocking the only exit. The shrouded figure eyed the device in Jim's hand and said, "So the rumors were true. Kanjigar, my . . . my *Trollhunter*, was felled. And the Amulet now belongs to the human standing in my smithy. I wonder, human, do these belong to you as well?"

The hooded Troll held out the droppers and foil wrappers from the oil baths. Jim recognized them as the kind of food coloring he'd use in his red velvet cake and the kind of antacid tablets his mom would give him when he had an upset stomach—usually after eating too much of that cake.

"Those are definitely from the surface world," said Jim. "But I swear, they're not ours."

"We hate littering too, but don't you think imprisonment is a bit of overkill?" added Toby.

"I'll ask the questions, instigator," said the hooded Troll.

"Stink gator?" AAARRRGGHH!!! asked in confusion.

"Instigator," corrected Blinky. "Another word for a troublemaker, inciter, or firebrand."

"And now, my *final* question," said the Troll in the hood. "Which of you killed my *son*?"

Jim and his friends looked from Draal's body in the corner of the cave to the Troll as she removed her hood. Blinky covered his mouth with all four of his hands and gasped, "Ballustra!"

The Monger Troll tossed her cloak to the side and leveled her crossbow at Team Trollhunters. Suddenly feeling very naked without his armor, Jim stepped in front of Toby and Claire and braced for the worst. But before Ballustra's finger could pull the crossbow trigger, an explosion rocked her blacksmith stall, shattering the worktable and all its contents. And for the second time that day, everything in Jim Lake Jr.'s world went completely black.

CHAPTER 8
HATCHING A PLAN

"Unending darkness," growled Gunmar the Gold. "This is what I herald."

Strickler heard the Gumm-Gumm's awful voice reverberate along the dry canal. He wasn't sure whether to run for his life or revert to his Changeling form and beg Gunmar for forgiveness. But Strickler decided to stay hidden behind the canal's tall, overgrown weeds. This choice ultimately proved to be a wise one, as two more figures emerged from the Horngazel.

"Lord Gunmar," said Queen Usurna, her engraved tattoos glowing in the shadow of the overhead bridge. "I would never question a leader as brutal and wise as you . . ."

Behind her, Angor Rot did his best to cover the

THE WAY OF THE WIZARD

disgust spreading across his pitted, crumbling face. The Troll assassin had spent two lifetimes battling— and now being forced to obey—Gunmar the Black, the Vicious, the Skullcrusher, or whatever other mad title he went by these days. As such, Angor Rot had seen firsthand just how impulsive and mercurial the one-eyed Gumm-Gumm could be. Brutal? Yes. But *wise*? Hardly.

Usurna chose her next words extremely carefully and said, "Yet, is this incursion onto the surface world advisable? You've just returned to Dark Trollmarket with Merlin's Staff of Avalon. You've uncovered Morgana's body at the very root of the Heartstone below us. Though she still remains incarcerated, the Eternal Night is within our grasp!"

"No thanks to you or your duplicitous ways, Usurna," spat Gunmar. "Never forget your place, which is beneath my heel, beside Angor Rot. And never forget how I, your Dark Underlord, have brought about the coming cataclysm single-handedly."

Angor Rot's scowl only intensified. *Single-handedly*. Absurd. Leeching all that power from the Heartstone had clearly made Gunmar delusional. How else could the "Dark Underlord" forget that Angor Rot had helped him secure the Staff of Avalon? That it had been Angor Rot himself who provided the borers—the tanklike drilling vehicles they used to travel to Merlin's Tomb? That while Gunmar was content to keep the Trollhunter's ally, Draal, alive as a mindless puppet, it was Angor Rot who had finally killed him? Or that Gunmar, in turn, had left Angor Rot for dead and taken one of the Borers back to Dark Trollmarket like some vainglorious conqueror?

After Angor Rot had crawled his way out of the geode pit, he'd vowed to return the favor. He had found the second Borer at the base of Merlin's Mountain, abandoned there by Gunmar just as Angor Rot had been. During the bedrock-breaking ride back to Dark Trollmarket, Angor Rot seethed. He fantasized of countless ways to slay Gunmar while the Borer's diamond-tipped drill bits tunneled through the Earth's crust. But by the time the vehicle returned to Dark Trollmarket's battered gyre station, Angor Rot had settled on a simple, elegant means of revenge. He would simply stab Gunmar in the back with his dagger and let the poisoned blade turn him into solid stone. Angor Rot would then break off pieces of Gunmar, toss them into the Borer, and watch the drills chew the "Dark Underlord" to dust.

Angor Rot had been just about to do it, too, when a chilling voice called to him once again. Morgana herself spoke directly into Angor Rot's soul from her prison in the Heartstone. Though her body had been trapped within the living crystal like a fly in amber, her will remained as domineering as ever. She ordered Angor Rot to stay his hand, just as she had granted him unbelievable power ages ago—power that came at a considerable cost.

Even from his hiding place, Strickler could see Angor Rot struggle to conceal his contempt for Gunmar. The Gumm-Gumm king breathed in the morning air, then bared his fangs at the acrid scents of car exhaust and other human pollutants. Gunmar spat black phlegm onto the canal floor and said, "The Eternal Night will exterminate the disgusting, pitiful creatures that have infested the surface world during my long absence. But first, these fleshlings must be made to suffer as I suffered in the Darklands. Bring forth . . . the eggs."

Strickler watched Angor Rot grudgingly do as

told. The Troll assassin opened the crate under his arm, revealing what looked like nine round, red rocks.

"Nyarlagroth eggs," gasped Usurna. "Were these smuggled out of the Darklands?"

"Those and many more," Gunmar said. "They made for tasty snacks upon my return. That is, until I rediscovered my appetite for human flesh. These nine eggs are all that remain."

The towering Gumm-Gumm now acknowledged Angor Rot's existence for the first time since they passed through the Horngazel. Gunmar studied Morgana's lackey for a moment, then said, "I recall you once had a way with animals, Angor Rot—perhaps because you are nothing more than an animal yourself. Awaken these sleeping beasts . . . or incur my wrath."

Angor Rot held Gunmar's stare for a moment before nodding in obedience. He arranged the nine eggs in a circle on the dry canal and began chanting, his voice low and guttural.

"Arune nagath," intoned Angor Rot. *"Nin sun nagath."*

Gunmar the Gold smiled malevolently. The red

shells splintered as Angor Rot continued in the old, forbidden tongue. And once his mantra stopped, a new noise replaced it. Nine blind Nyarlagroths hatched from their eggs and took their first breaths. The mewling eel-like creatures screeched and uncoiled to their full lengths of about three feet each.

"Gunmar, no Nyarlagroth has ever trod upon the surface lands," Usurna cautioned. "Who knows what effects their presence here might wreak!"

"*I* know," said Gunmar, picking up one of the Nyarlagroths and permitting it to slither between his claws. "And so should you. As a deep-cave Krubera Troll, your knowledge of this world's subterranean structure should be second to none."

Usurna's feathered headdress trembled with the rest of her body when she considered the full implications of Gunmar's statement. She steeled herself and said, "This human city rests on an active fault line—a fissure where two tectonic plates meet. If these Nyarlagroths should burrow beneath Arcadia as they do in the Darklands, it would trigger—"

"An earthquake," Strickler whispered to himself in horror.

"The fleshlings' suffering will be so absolute, they shall beg me to slaughter them even before the advent of the Eternal Night," said Gunmar.

He returned the baby Nyarlagroth to the rest of the litter and stomped on the ground, breaking the concrete. The vibrations startled the sightless eels, making them scurry through the crack at Gunmar's hooves. Behind the weeds, Strickler swallowed nervously. He could feel the juvenile Nyarlagroths tunneling under and past him already.

And behind Gunmar, Angor Rot reconsidered his earlier position. Yes, the Gumm-Gumm king was clearly brutal. But in seeing how cleverly he plotted this new wave of destruction, Angor Rot conceded that Gunmar the Gold might indeed be wise as well. Yet this was not the wisdom of a teacher or sorcerer.

This was the wisdom of a maniac.

CHAPTER 9
WORLD WAR TROLL

The Amulet may not have been able to conjure any armor around its Trollhunter. But at the moment, it made for a pretty handy flashlight. Jim used its faint blue glow to search the rubble around him. Although he couldn't see what happened after that explosion struck Ballustra's smithy, Jim certainly *heard* its walls come down around him and his friends.

"Claire! Tobes! Blinky! AAARRRGGHH!!!" Jim called. "Let me know you're okay—PLEASE!"

By way of answer, the debris beneath Jim's sneakers shifted. He jumped out of the way just as AAARRRGGHH!!! burst out of the ruins. Holding up tons of rock, the gentle giant made a path for Toby, Claire, Blinky, and Merlin to emerge unscathed.

"I didn't hear you call *my* name in concern," Merlin said as Jim hugged his friends.

With everyone now clear, Jim canvassed the remainder of the cave and discovered that Ballustra was gone. He also found Draal's overturned body lying on its side amidst the scattered wreckage of the smithy. One piece had been knocked loose from the statue and gleamed in the Amulet's glow— Draal's nose ring. Jim pocketed it as another deafening detonation thundered nearby.

"Why, it sounds as if a veritable Troll war erupted just beyond this cavern!" said Blinky.

"A war? Here? Right after Draal's mom accused us of instigating trouble?" Claire said skeptically. "Doesn't that seem a little too coincidental to anyone else?"

Merlin gave Claire a knowing wink and tapped the side of his nose, as if she was onto something. Watching the Amulet pulse in his hand, Jim reminded himself that, when it came to Trollhunting, there was no such thing as coincidence.

"Only destiny," Jim uttered to no one in particular.

"What's that, Master Jim?" asked Blinky, not quite hearing him.

"This has been a seriously messed-up day, and I seriously need to hit something," answered Jim. "What better place to do that than a battlefield?"

The rest of Team Trollhunters and Merlin followed Jim as he marched out of the blasted blacksmith stall and down a tunnel choked with more fallen rocks. Before long, the path widened into an antechamber, and the sounds of conflict rang louder than ever. Turning the last corner, Jim looked out at an immense cavern—where an equally immense civil war between the Garden Trolls and River Trolls was underway.

Boulders flew. Dwärkstone grenades blasted into shrapnel. And rival Trolls collided against one another on the front lines like pawns on a bloody chessboard. Spurred on by their Ruler, the River Trolls dug deep trenches in the ground, exposing underground streams. The water shot out of the ruts like the stream from a fire hose, knocking back the enemy infantry. In retaliation, the Garden Trolls joined their Elder as he bade wild, twisting plant roots to punch out of the earth and ensnare the River tribe's strongest warriors.

Jim and the others could barely process the full

scope of this crazed conflict. Except Merlin. The wizard simply shook his head wearily, as if he'd seen this type of thing happen far, far too many times before. Claire's eyes scanned the various fronts, then widened when they spotted someone smack-dab at the center of the conflict. She pointed straight ahead and said, "There!"

The team followed Claire's line of sight to a middle ground in the sodden, vine-strewn combat zone. There, Ballustra distributed various weapons—similar in design to her crossbow—to the River Trolls. In return, the boulder-topped soldiers handed over purses filled with gems.

"Unbelievable!" Jim roared. "She's an arms dealer!"

Blinky placed a calming hand on the Trollhunter's shoulder and said, "Master Jim, you must understand. Ballustra is a Monger Troll. It is in her very nature to construct and disperse arms to those who wage war."

"Her *nature*?!" cried Jim. "Blink, Ballustra's own son just died, and she's conducting *business* in the middle of a battlefield and—wait a minute. Is she selling to the *other side* now?"

He indicated Ballustra's weapons bazaar, which had now moved to the Garden Trolls' camp. As she bartered more of her bolas and double-headed axes for bushels of glowing tubers and jugs of resin, Jim said, "What about that seems in any way *natural* to you?"

"Actually, gang, I don't even know if nature has anything to do with it," Toby chimed in. "Look who else crashed World War Troll!"

Toby jerked his thumb to the other end of the cavern, where Porgon delighted in fanning the flames. Skulking in the periphery, he brushed his glowing hex arm against one of the River Trolls' water bazookas, causing it to backfire and soak its handlers. The Trickster Troll then stealthily grazed one of the Garden Trolls' vines, making it snake around their Elder and throttle him. Porgon positively overflowed with giggles, yet none of the fighting Trolls noticed him amid the chaos. None noticed him save for the members of Team Trollhunters.

"Stink gator," said AAARRRGGHH!!!

"A most appropriate appraisal, my friend," Blinky agreed. "Though the River and Garden Troll feud is the stuff of legend, Porgon's presence here only serves to foment more hostility."

"Oh?" asked Merlin. "You've encountered this Porgon cretin before?"

"Yeah, back in Arcadia, right before Jim skewered him with the Sword of Daylight," said Claire. "We figured that was the end of Porgon . . . only now I'm starting to understand why he's called a Trickster Troll."

Blinky's eyebrows arched as he said, "In point of fact, the Trickster Trolls were the very same charlatans who created the Glamour Masks we've employed of late. It is conceivable he used one such mask to make another, hapless Troll appear like him while the *real* Porgon made quick his escape!"

"You mean he pulled a switcheroo, and Jim eighty-sixed the wrong Troll?" Toby wailed.

"Sadly, it would appear so," conceded Blinky.

"And it would appear I've found something to hit," said Jim.

Despite his lack of armor, the Trollhunter rolled up his sleeves and marched headlong into the battle. Claire, Toby, Blinky, and AAARRRGGHH!!! scrambled after him, while Merlin went back to shaking his head.

"Master Jim, with all due respect, have you completely lost your mind?" Blinky cried, dashing past wrestling Garden and River Trolls.

Jim may not have had his sword or shield, but he still knew how to move during a battle. He ducked the blast of a water jet and somersaulted over a tangle of sentient roots. Toby extended his Warhammer and swung it back and forth to keep oncoming Troll soldiers at a distance, while AAARRRGGHH!!! did the same with his fists. Claire rushed up to Jim and forced him to stop in his tracks.

"Jim, this isn't like you!" she said. "Taking out your anger on someone—even someone as terrible as Porgon—isn't going to change things. It isn't going to bring back Draal."

Jim looked into Claire's wide, searching eyes. In that moment, he wished he could give anything—even *his* own right arm—to make their lives return to the way they were just a week ago.

"Master Jim, watch out!" yelled Blinky.

His six eyes spied Porgon recognizing the Trollhunter from a few feet away. The Trickster Troll tittered with more laughter and hurled a spell with his enchanted arm. Blinky shoved Jim clear just before the hex hit Blinky, AAARRRGGHH!!!, Toby, and Claire. Satisfied with his mischief for the moment, Porgon scampered away. But his spell drew the attention of several River and Garden Trolls in the vicinity. The bruised grunts spotted Team Trollhunters. Yet when the hex's smoke cleared, their eyes saw something entirely different.

"Four more River Trolls, in our midst!" said one of the Garden Troll soldiers.

"Wha—?! A quartet of Garden Troll interlopers!" said one of the River Trolls.

But both were talking about the same four figures—Blinky, AAARRRGGHH!!!, Toby, and Claire. As the two armies closed in on them, Blinky said, "It would appear Porgon's glamours aren't limited to masks! He's made us look like River Trolls to the Garden tribe—"

"And like Garden Trolls to the River tribe!" Claire finished, catching on fast.

"Not good," said AAARRRGGHH!!! as he avoided swipes from both sides.

"Since Claire's Shadow Staff is out of order,

74

everyone buddy up around me!" said Toby.

The friends grabbed onto his Warhammer, and Toby concentrated, levitating all four of them out of the River and Garden Trolls' reach. As they floated up toward the cavern's domed ceiling, Toby, Claire, Blinky, and AAARRRGGHH!!! saw Jim getting to his feet again. They all wanted to go back for him, yet they knew the spell affecting their appearances would only endanger Jim. Drifting away, Claire took one last look back, seeing Merlin's emerald figure stroll between the battlefronts and up to Jim. She wasn't sure if this was a good thing or not.

"Merlin, you're a wizard," said Jim, his voice surprisingly restrained. "You know magic, even without your staff. Can't you help my friends? Or make my Amulet—*your* Amulet—work? Or, or, or—just bring Draal back to life? Please? I . . . I'm begging you here. Please."

Merlin regarded the boy before him in a new light. He seemed to consider Jim's plea, taking each impassioned word to heart. And Jim's own heart skipped a beat when he saw Merlin smile, when he believed the wizard would actually grant his wish. Clearing his throat, Merlin adopted a kind expression and said, "Give a man a fish, and you feed him for a day—"

"What," Jim said flatly. "Are you serious right now? Why can't you just give me a straight answer for once? If you're so magical and smart and important, why can't you just stop all this—this Troll war, the Eternal Night, my friends dying—*all of it* on your own?"

The wizard waited for Jim to finish, then resumed saying, ". . . but *teach* a man to fish, and you feed him for a lifetime."

The Trollhunter lowered his head in resignation, only vaguely aware of the war gradually moving away from him. Merlin paced in a circle around his young champion and said, "I can see that you're trying to strike a deal. Much like Ballustra with her weapon sales. And I was not unaware of your anger earlier, nor your disbelief upon awakening." Would it surprise you to know that I'm glad you're experiencing these emotions this strongly—this quickly?"

Jim looked up and glared at the wizard, confusion clouding his blue eyes. The wizard let out a weary sigh and said, "This is why I decided that we would walk back to your home. And why I didn't rush to free you from those shackles. To give you the time to get your feelings in order, boy. Had I let your comely lass shadow-jump us to Arcadia Oaks straightaway—and had I let my Trollhunter go up against Gunmar in his present state—you'd wind up deader than your late compatriot, Draal. So, y'know, you're welcome."

"You know what? I'm changing my wish," said Jim. "My new wish is to hear some *real* advice from a *real* hero, like Kanjigar the Courageous. Not pointless proverbs from some washed-up old wizard."

"Okeydoke," said Merlin before waving a hand and making his Trollhunter disappear.

CHAPTER 10
TO BE, OR NOTENRIQUE TO BE

"Oh dear! And *then* what happened?" asked Nana Domzalski.

She adjusted her incredibly thick glasses before spooning cat food out of a tin can and into a porcelain thimble. Nana pushed the thimble across her kitchen table, and Chompsky took it into his tiny hand before remembering his manners. He turned and gallantly offered the first bite to the Sally-Go-Back action figure beside him. Despite her twenty points of articulation, Sally remained perfectly still. Chompsky shrugged and started chowing down all by himself.

"Neep, *neep* neep," he said between nibbles, looking lovingly into Sally's plastic eyes.

"I just love hearing stories of how couples met,"

Nana said while pouring hot tea into two cups. "You know, Toby's grandpa and I caused quite a stir when we first got together."

"Neep?" inquired Chompsky.

"Everyone had an opinion about us," Nana said, her gummy mouth curling into a nostalgic grin. "In the end, our love outlasted all the naysayers . . . even if my Horace didn't."

"What drivel," muttered Dictatious from the corner. "A Gnome and a doll?! My vision may have failed me of late, but even *I* can see this 'relationship' is doomed."

"Sounds like someone's a little jealous," Nana tittered behind her teacup.

Chompsky joined in giggling, gently elbowing Sally-Go-Back to see if she got the joke too. Sally just stared ahead, smiling pleasantly. Ignoring them, Dictatious sniffed the scent of the tea. He fumbled toward the table and grabbed the second teacup with his four hands. The Troll breathed in the aroma deeply . . . before dumping the tea on the floor and biting into the saucer with a satisfying crunch.

Oblivious to the destruction of her fine china,

Nana once again pushed her glasses up the bridge of her nose and said, "This isn't about seeing with your eyes. It's about seeing with your heart. And I've got a good feeling these two lovebirds are gonna make it!"

Chompsky gave Sally a kiss on her clear helmet, then went bashful at this public display of affection. Everyone was in such good spirits at the moment—everyone except Dictatious, that is—they failed to notice how Nana's tea started to ripple in her cup. . . .

"What a disgrace," said NotEnrique, his two yellow eyes narrowed in disgust. "I mean, lookit ya. Talkin' nonsense all the time. Stinkin' up the house. Fallin' flat on yer face whenever ya take more than two steps. For the love a' Gorgus, don't ya have any self-respect?"

The real Enrique gurgled in delight at the small Changeling perched on his crib like a gargoyle. With drool-lacquered hands, the baby reached out and grabbed two fistfuls of NotEnrique's fur.

"Hey, watch me scruff!" NotEnrique wailed. "I'm not one a yer stuffed animals!"

The green imp shoved away the hands, losing a

few tufts of hair in the process. Enrique's lips quivered in abrupt sadness. Tears started to well in his enormous eyes.

"Aw swell, here come the waterworks," the Changeling said in exasperation. "Isn't that rich! I lose the ability ta change me appearance soon as the Trollhunter rescues ya from the Darklands, and *you're* the one who's about ta cry. Whatta hypocrite. . . ."

He ignored Enrique's fussy whimpers and looked around at their nursery. Colorful alphabet blocks and plush toys filled the shelves. Mobiles twirled lazily from the ceiling. And sunlight poured through the windows, lending the entire room a cheery glow. NotEnrique sighed heavily and said, "I used ta have a sweet racket goin' here. Comfy crib, regular feedings, baby wipe warmer . . . I used ta have a place in the surface world. A reason for bein'."

NotEnrique's eyes softened, settling on a framed photo of Claire cuddling with her little brother. Well, Claire and her parents had *assumed* that was Enrique when they took the picture months ago. But NotEnrique remembered the visit to the photography studio at the Arcadia Oaks Mall as if it were yesterday. The thought of it brought a weak smile to the Changeling's face, even as he started to sniffle.

"Used ta have it all," NotEnrique said through his congestion. "Until *you* came back, you . . . you . . ."

Only now did NotEnrique become aware of the insistent tugging on his diaper. He looked down at the baby clinging to his bottom. Enrique offered up his pacifier to the pint-sized Changeling. NotEnrique took it and said, "You want me ta have this?"

"Baba," said Enrique.

"Er, thanks, but no thanks, short stuff," said NotEnrique, handing back the pacifier. "I don't need to add a case of hand, hoot, and mouth disease to me pile o' woes."

"BABA!" Enrique yelled.

"All right, already!" NotEnrique yelled back.

He jammed the baba into his mouth to prevent one of Enrique's temper tantrums. The pacifier's curdled taste made NotEnrique want to spit it out and curse at the baby some more. But after a second or two, the flavor mellowed, and NotEnrique discovered that the pacifier left him feeling strangely . . . pacified. Enrique then pulled out a matching baba from somewhere inside his onesie and popped it into his own mouth. The two of them sat at opposite sides of the crib, staring at each other and enjoying their babas—human and Changeling, infant and impostor, Enrique and NotEnrique.

A moment later, NotEnrique felt the mattress vibrate under their bottoms. He cast a suspicious look at the baby and said, "I don't care that we're havin' a moment. If ya just went boom-boom in yer diaper, I ain't changin' it!"

The vibrations increased in their intensity, now overtaking the entire room. Toys toppled from the shelves, and the framed portrait of Claire and her *hermanito* shattered. The door flung open, and a panicked Javier and Ophelia raced into the nursery. But they skidded to a halt at the sight of their son and his green decoy in the same crib. NotEnrique spit out his baba and said, "Look, I know we started off on the wrong hoof, but how would ya like bein' the proud parents of *twins*?"

"This . . . this is the most disturbing thing I've ever witnessed in my life," said Ophelia.

"Maybe we *should* have left Enrique in day care," said Javier.

They pulled Enrique away from the Changeling as the tremors multiplied. Feeling jilted as well as jolted, NotEnrique hopped out of the crib and onto the windowsill. He took one look outside and said, "I think we're all 'bout ta get disturbed—big-time!"

Two blocks away, Barbara Lake felt the same temblors beneath her home. As pots and pans fell onto the kitchen floor, Barbara dashed to the nearest doorframe for safety, although her own well-being was the farthest thing from her mind at the moment. She kept thinking about Jim, about how crushed he sounded before their call cut out. Barbara wished Jim were here so that she could hug him, not the doorframe, during—

"This isn't an earthquake!" Strickler shouted as he barged in through the front door.

He joined her under the doorframe and, for the first time ever, Walt appeared disheveled to Barbara. His hair was mussed, his clothes rumpled, and sweat beaded his face, as if he'd just run across town—which he had. After watching Gunmar, Usurna, and Angor Rot return to Dark Trollmarket through the Horngazel portal, Strickler had raced to the museum. But he'd apparently missed Nomura by mere minutes, and his frantic phone calls to her cell were met by a full voice-mail inbox. And so Strickler was forced to opt for plan *B*—or plan *C*, as it were. A new wave of tremors brought Strickler back into the present, and he said, "This is Gunmar's work!"

Barbara's eyes widened in alarm before a savvy look overtook her face. She took a step back from Strickler and said, "Is that so? And I'm just supposed to, what, be thankful you're here? To save me from the big, bad world after all?"

"I know you don't trust me," Strickler admitted. "But if you won't accept my help, then I hope you'll at least accept protection from *them*."

Steve Palchuk and Eli Pepperjack stepped into the Lake household. Wearing their all-black uniforms and helmets, they checked behind furniture and around corners for enemy agents that simply weren't there.

"Elijah?" said Barbara in surprise. "Stevie?"

"It's, uh, Steve now," he replied. "Nobody's

called me 'Stevie' since kindergarten."

"And we're on duty, Dr. Lake," added Eli. "So please refer to us as . . . *the Creepslayerz!*"

Barbara didn't know which sounded worse— that ridiculous code name, or the bone-chilling roars that now echoed under her front yard.

CHAPTER 11
LOCKED HORNS

One second ago, Jim had been standing in the middle of a wet, weed-choked battlefield. But now he found himself in the middle of a misty expanse without borders, time, or direction.

"The Void," Jim said to himself.

"For one who still lives, you make an inordinate number of appearances in our afterlife, Trollhunter," greeted a familiar voice.

Jim saw an incandescent orb zooming through the haze toward him. The energy sphere then unfurled and assumed the ghostly form of his predecessor, Kanjigar the Courageous. Although they'd never met in life, Kanjigar had grown fond of Jim ever since Merlin's Amulet passed between them. From this ethereal realm, the previous Trollhunter had watched with great admiration as Jim trained under old friends like Blinky and AAARRRGGHH!!!, valorously shouldering the responsibilities of the human and Troll worlds alike.

"I hadn't expected to see you again for quite some time, now that Gunmar has taken over Trollmarket, and the Soothscryer within it," Kanjigar added while holding out a hand.

But Jim sidestepped the handshake and hugged Kanjigar, startling the transparent Troll with the fervor of his embrace. Jim finally let go, wiped his eyes, and said, "Kanjigar, I'm so sorry, but Draal . . . he . . . ."

"My son is dead," Kanjigar said, sparing Jim the onus of uttering the words himself.

"You knew," Jim realized. "Of course you did. You can see everything from the Void. Then . . . you also saw how it's my fault. Draal gave up his life so I could keep mine. But it was such a waste. Just because I've survived this long doesn't mean I deserve to be the Trollhunter."

Gone were the mirth and youthful brio that always flickered behind Jim's eyes whenever Kanjigar would surveil him from the afterlife. Instead, a deep and somber sadness seemed to have taken root in his teenage heart. Kanjigar extended his hand again, this time clasping it about Jim's armored shoulder.

"Heed my words, Trollhunter, for they are the truth," said Kanjigar. "Had Draal wielded Daylight in your place, the Eternal Night would've occurred months ago. Make no mistake, I love my son. Yet it is you—and you alone—who keeps that apocalypse at bay, Jim Lake Jr."

"But he looked up to you, and you were the greatest champion of all!" argued Jim.

"Said the living Trollhunter to the ghost," Kanjigar replied.

Jim felt like he should probably laugh. But the heavy weight pressing on his belly, heart, and lungs made such a thing seem impossible. Kanjigar must've sensed this, for he then said, "I jest, of course. Yet my point remains. Since the day he was born, I have known that Draal would die young. Well, young for a *Troll*."

Just as instantaneously as Jim wound up in the Void, he now found himself transported to a place he'd seen only once before—Glastonbury Tor Trollmarket. Nestled deep below the English moors, this underground city resembled the Trollmarket beneath Arcadia, save for the purple Heartstone that jutted from the ceiling like an overgrown stalactite.

"This is another of those Void Visitations, isn't it?" Jim asked aloud.

Kanjigar nodded and released the Trollhunter's shoulder. Jim felt so melancholy, so drained, he didn't even want to take a step. Yet his ghostly guide ushered them to this Trollmarket's version of the Hero's Forge. Hearing the clang of swords and the whoosh of fire, Jim looked over the edge and saw none other than—

"Draal!" Jim exclaimed, though no one other than Kanjigar's spirit heard him.

But there was Draal the Deadly training in the pit, sparring with automated blades, dodging blasts of flame that shot from the floor. Off to the side, Jim saw another Kanjigar—this one also very much alive—paying more attention to the scroll in his hands than to Draal's practice.

"That's you, before you became a Trollhunter," Jim said to the ghost. "That means—"

"Aye, we're in the past, before Trolls even

traveled to your country," Kanjigar's spirit confirmed. "Yet some things never change."

Taking a closer look at the Hero's Forge, Jim understood what Kanjigar meant. This Draal was younger than the one Jim had befriended, and he had not yet taken to wearing a nose ring. But it became immediately apparent that Draal, at any age, lived to fight. The spiked Troll rolled through the remainder of his obstacle course and, with his chest still heaving from the exertion, said, "Father, did you see? I cleared the trials in less time than it took this morning—a new record! Are you not proud?"

Jim watched the living Kanjigar pull himself away from his scroll long enough to say, "I'd be prouder if you'd put even half as much effort into your studies."

"But, Father, I never feel so alive as when I am in combat," Draal replied.

"Combat cares not for those who are alive, my son," said Kanjigar. "Only for death."

"Then I hope I should be so lucky as to meet a glorious death on the field of battle," Draal huffed before rolling out of the Hero's Forge in anger.

Jim looked from the living Kanjigar to the ghostly

one at his side. He noticed how they both wore the same troubled, inevitable expression.

"Draal must've inherited that temper from his mom," Jim guessed.

"You have no idea, Trollhunter," sighed Kanjigar's spirit. "Indeed, Ballustra and I often locked horns over how to raise our son. In the end, we came to the conclusion that we'd fare better as parents if we went our separate ways."

Jim watched Kanjigar watching his younger self, who was still engrossed with his scroll, and felt sympathy for both of them. The Trollhunter said, "I'm sorry, Kanjigar. I had no idea."

"Nor did I," the spirit said as he forced a smile. "As a result, I spent far too long feeling . . . well, feeling the way you do now."

Jim broke off eye contact and took stock of his own emotions. He hadn't really comprehended the depth of his own sorrow until someone else pointed it out to him.

"Take heart, Trollhunter," added Kanjigar. "It will get better. With time . . ."

Once again, Jim's surroundings shifted. He now stood in Ballustra's smithy—the very same cave Jim had just seen demolished by the Troll civil war. Yet it still appeared intact in this Void Visitation, and Jim and Kanjigar observed as young Draal spoke with his mother.

"Then your decision is final?" Ballustra asked.

"It is," answered Draal. "I fear for Father's safety. The 'New World' is no place for a scholar. If he is to join Deya in her quest to find a new Heartstone, then he will need protection."

"I, for one, can think of no greater—or deadlier— protector than my son," said Ballustra with a somber smile. "Though I shall miss him more than he could ever know."

"Mother, come with us," Draal said.

"Alas, I cannot," said Ballustra, blinking away tears. "My place is here, in my smithy, building the weapons needed to defend those Trolls who, like me, choose to stay behind. Just as your place is beside Kanjigar. Yet, perhaps some small part of me might still travel with you. . . ."

Ballustra unfastened her nose ring and handed it to Draal. He took the engraved heirloom and inserted it into his own snout. Jim felt his pocket, where that same ring now rested, before a thick veil of mist passed in front of his eyes. When it cleared, he and Kanjigar were back in the Void. His chest and mind feeling clearer than they had before the visitation, Jim said, "Blinky told us about what happened next. About how you became the next Trollhunter on the way to America. About the Great Rocky Mountain Troll War you fought there. And about how Draal really did protect you the entire time. You may not have *needed* that protection anymore, but it sounded like you were both exactly where you needed to be."

Kanjigar said, "Perhaps we might say the same of you in this moment. With my dying breath, I begged Merlin to spare Draal from becoming the Trollhunter. To let him have a life of his own, not one defined by the wants of an Amulet or a distracted parent. The wizard answered my wish, just as he answered your wish to speak with me."

Jim ran his hand through his hair, reconsidering. Hearing Kanjigar put it this way, Jim now wondered if that cranky old wizard didn't just clonk-donk him to the Void out of spite. Maybe there was a method to Merlin's madness after all.

"And yet, I now see in death what I couldn't in

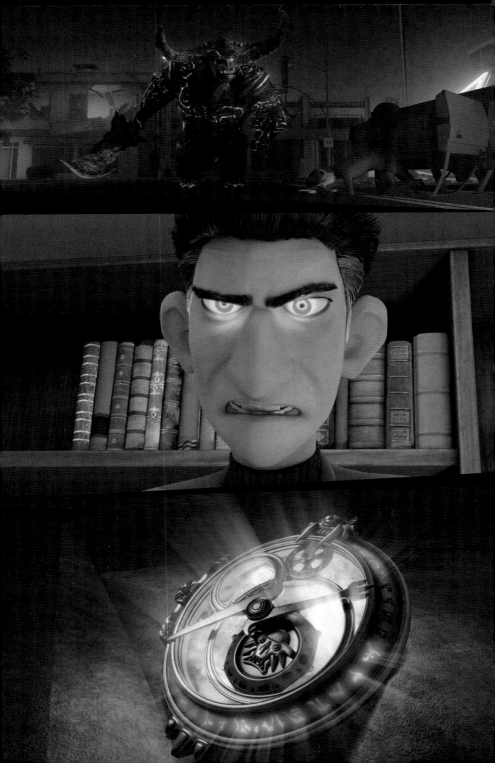

life," Kanjigar continued. "That each of us, human and Troll alike, must walk our own path, some paths shorter than others."

Galvanized by the purity behind Kanjigar's words, Jim raised his head and looked into his predecessor's ghostly eyes. Kanjigar placed a fist over his Amulet and said, "You need not feel guilt, Trollhunter, nor need you grieve my son any longer. If you wish to honor him, then honor him by continuing what he loved most in life. Make peace with your heart, get back on your path, and, for the glory of Draal the Deadly—FIGHT."

CHAPTER 12
THE O.P.

"Just hang a little longer, guys—we're almost there!" Toby hollered unconvincingly.

He felt his grip on the Warhammer slip and saw that Claire, Blinky, and AAARRRGGHH!!! all struggled to cling onto the floating mallet, too. They'd all been hovering over the warring Garden and River Trolls for what seemed like hours, though it was likely closer to minutes. In that time, all of their arms had grown fatigued. But Toby spotted an empty muddy stretch at the outskirts of the battlefield. If they could just make it there and rest for a moment, Blinky would definitely be able to come up with some sort of plan to—

"Incoming!" Claire shouted.

A regiment of River Trolls launched a gigantic river stone from one of Ballustra's trebuchets. As the boulder catapulted toward Team Trollhunters, Toby's mind raced.

"Um, everyone ignore what I just said! In fact, do the opposite—let go!" he yelped.

All four friends released the Warhammer and plunged to the ground, more than fifty feet below them. As they fell, Blinky grabbed Toby and Claire right before AAARRRGGHH!!! wrapped his body around all three of them.

With a gigantic splat, AAARRRGGHH!!! landed back-first into the mud. He unfurled his arms, and Blinky, Claire, and Toby—dazed, but otherwise unharmed—slipped onto the squishy mire. The unmanned Warhammer plopped beside them, and AAARRRGGHH!!! shook the muck from his fur, splattering the others. Blinky wiped the grime from his six eyes and said, "We're fortunate the River Trolls soaked this terrain so thoroughly; it made for a soft landing. To say nothing of the way Tobias carried us here by sheer willpower—even a Troll of AAARRRGGHH!!!'s considerable carriage!"

"Aw, he ain't heavy, he's my wingman," Toby said with a muddy fist bump.

"Garden Troll filth!" shouted a nearby voice.

They spun around and recognized the regiment that had shot them down. Five River Trolls surrounded Toby, Claire, Blinky, and AAARRRGGHH!!!, pointing more of Ballustra's signature weapons at them. Team Trollhunters huddled defensively, and Blinky whispered, "It would seem this mud has done little to conceal Porgon's glamour over all of us!"

"Who are you calling filth, river rat?" shouted a Garden Troll.

Team Trollhunters spun around again and found a company of five Garden Trolls cornering them from the other side, brandishing even more of Ballustra's weapons. Their leader pointed his pitchfork at the four muddy figures and said, "We claim *all* of you River Trolls as our prisoners of war!"

AAARRRGGHH!!!, Blinky, Toby, and Claire each braced for a fight, when they heard someone clear his throat with a deliberate "Ahem." The group spun around a third time and saw Merlin approaching, careful not to get any mud on his emerald boots. Claire looked beyond the wizard, seeing he was alone, and asked, "Where's Jim? Wasn't he with you?"

"The Trollhunter needed a time-out," said the

wizard. "And so does this little charade."

With a snap of his fingers, Porgon's glamour dissipated. Toby, Claire, Blinky, and AAARRRGGHH!!! stood revealed as two humans and two Trolls. The River and Garden soldiers spluttered, then glowered with renewed suspicion at each other.

"Don't be daft," said Merlin. "This level of trickery's beyond your tribes' ken."

"Then who?" demanded a Garden Troll. "Who pulled the moss over our eyes?"

"Likely the same trickster who suggested you reconnoiter this particular area and who ordered the River Trolls to fire their catapult at that particular moment," said Merlin.

The wizard snapped his fingers once more, and the muck at his feet magically sculpted into an incredibly lifelike bust of Porgon. Merlin said, "Look familiar?"

The River and Garden Trolls shook their heads. *Nope.*

"How about now?" Merlin asked, reshaping the mud to add a boulder atop the head.

"It's him!" cried one of the River Trolls. "He calibrated our catapult's aim!"

"As I suspected," Merlin sighed, altering the

head so that branches now adorned it.

"That's the one who supplied our camp with Grave Sand!" said a Garden Troll. "The stuff's whipping our forces into a frenzy!"

"Porgon's been playing both sides against each other!" Claire realized. "And who knows for how long. . . ."

"Why don't we just ask him?" said Merlin. "He's right over there."

Merlin pointed at one of the five River Trolls and vanished the boulder atop his head and the algae beard along his chin—revealing Porgon beneath the disguise. He burst into another giggle, this one a tad more high-pitched and nervous than usual.

"Think you can out-trick a Trickster Troll, do you?" taunted Porgon.

Merlin blew a rather unimpressed raspberry and said, "Please. You address the fellow who *invented* pranks."

With his hexing arm, Porgon tapped an unsuspecting River Troll. The soldier then involuntarily spat out a mouthful of river water at Merlin. Without batting an eye, the wizard doffed his skullcap. The curved headpiece caught the stream and redirected it—right into Porgon's face.

"Touché!" Blinky hailed from the sidelines.

The Trickster Troll shook the water from his mug, then hexed a Garden Troll before she could avoid his touch. Her branches suddenly burst into flames, and she ran around in distress like a fiery bull. Merlin yawned, grabbed ahold of Claire's sleeves, and said, "May I?"

Before Claire could say no, he removed her blazer, turned it inside out, and changed the color of the lining to a bright red. The wizard held out the crimson coat like a matador's cape. As the Garden Troll passed by, he twirled the jacket with a flourish, making her disappear.

"Whoa!" said Toby, Claire, Blinky, and AAARRRGGHH!!! in unison.

Everyone wondered what had happened to that hexed Garden Troll—until she appeared again behind Porgon. Still barreling ahead in a straight line, the Garden Troll rammed the trickster's backside with her lit branches. Porgon jumped into the air, gripping his singed hindquarters, and landed face-first in a pool of mud.

Smirking, Merlin poured the leftover river water

from his skullcap onto the Garden Troll's branches. The flames extinguished, only to be replaced by a fresh bloom of leaves. The other Garden and River Trolls couldn't help but applaud, drawing the attention of nearby soldiers from both sides. A larger crowed gathered as the wizard extended an armored hand to Porgon and said, "No hard feelings?"

The Trickster Troll took Merlin's hand—only for it to pop off Merlin's wrist. Porgon lost his balance, winding up with more mud on his face and an empty gauntlet in his grip.

"Ah, the old false hand gag," chuckled Merlin, wiggling his armored fingers as if they'd never left his arm. "Never gets old."

While Porgon's feet struggled to find purchase on the slippery sludge, he heard giggles. But they were not his own, for a change. Droves of River and Garden Trolls had given up their battles to join in laughing at him. They all stood side by side, pointing and jeering at the outclassed and out-pranked Porgon.

"Stop it!" the Trickster Troll demanded. "You're supposed to laugh *with* me, not *at* me!"

But this just made the Troll audience laugh even louder. Merlin raised his hands in the air, silencing the crowd, and said, "Though he may look the buffoon at present, I believe Porgon to be the chief architect behind your perpetual feud—and all for his own amusement!"

The gathered Trolls did not appear to be in a laughing mood anymore. They turned their angry eyes upon Porgon, who shrieked, "Lies! The wizard lies! Yes, I may have nudged both tribes a little here and there. But a Trickster Troll never acts directly. I merely added fuel to the animosity already burning betwixt your camps!"

The assembled Garden and River Trolls now noticed how closely they had become intermingled. They started to shove at one another. Then came the swinging fists, followed by more volleys of vegetation and water. Team Trollhunters ducked away from the renewed war, and Blinky said, "So much for an armistice."

"Army sis?" asked AAARRRGGHH!!!

"Armistice," Blinky corrected. "It means ceasefire, suspension of hostilities, a truce."

"But if Merlin couldn't broker one, then who can?" asked Claire.

A portal tore open in front of them. Pale blue

vapor cascaded out of the breach, followed by one metal boot, then another. The mists parted, and Jim appeared, clad in the gleaming Daylight Armor. As his friends embraced their returned Trollhunter, Jim said to Merlin, "Thanks. I needed that."

"A mere parlor trick," the wizard muttered with a dismissive wave.

"Don't sell yourself short, Merlin," Toby said. "You're the O.P.—original pranksta!"

"I see the war's still raging," said Jim of the strife sprawling around them.

"Indeed, Master Jim," Blinky said. "It's as if every Troll refuses to stop fighting!"

"Then it's a good thing we don't need every Troll to stop fighting," Jim said with sudden clarity. "Just one."

CHAPTER 13
PUZZLE PRINCE

Gold-and-black talons picked up a pebble and inserted it between two larger stones. The pieces fit perfectly, like the tiles in a mosaic.

Gunmar took a step back to judge his progress so far. He supposed the Heartstone around him had likely glowed brighter when these private quarters belonged to that fool Vendel. But now that black streaks of rot coursed through it, Trollmarket's luster had diminished considerably. Still, the corrupted crystal gave enough light for Gunmar to see his subject take shape.

"My, my," echoed a lilting voice from the shadows.

Gunmar stood erect. Behind him, the Heartstone's decayed veins wove into the silhouette of a severe woman in a barbed headdress. She clucked her tongue and said, "In all my years, I've only seen you destroy, never create. Perhaps I should take to calling you Gunmar the *Artiste*?"

"Morgana," Gunmar said to the living shade. "You grace me with your malign presence."

"Do I?" said Morgana from behind the Heartstone barrier. "I'd have thought you were avoiding me, the way you hide in here alone, playing with little toy rocks."

"Hiding?" Gunmar roared. "I hide from no one!"

"Then how else do you explain your inaction?" Morgana said with a disapproving *tsk*.

Gunmar's eye wandered to Merlin's Staff of Avalon. It leaned against the corner of Vendel's onetime workshop, its green gemstone pulsing faintly in the dark.

"Only that staff can free me from my prison within this very Heartstone," said Morgana. "Did you think I spent so many centuries in here, I wouldn't mind another day more? While you waste time reassembling your puzzle prince?"

Gunmar considered his work-in-progress. In the faint half-light of the Heartstone, the remains of Gunmar's son, Bular, stood rebuilt into some patchwork monument to brutality, pebble by miserable pebble. The Dark Underlord studied the cracks marring Bular's reconstructed face. Finally, he said, "I already tried to free you from your chrysalis with the staff, Pale Lady, but the effort was for naught. Rather than try the same fruitless tactic twice, I chose to come here and plot my next move."

"A most sound explanation," Morgana said. "Was it meant to convince me . . . or yourself?"

For the first time in his long, torturous existence, Gunmar hesitated. But the silence quickly abated, when the ceiling rumbled above them. Recovering from his delay, Gunmar pointed a razor-sharp finger upward and said, "Neither. The nine Nyarlagroths speak to my conviction. Listen how they grow, Eldritch Queen, how their movements have sewn disarray in long, ugly scars beneath the surface world. The Trollhunter—*if* his puny human heart still beats—shall be too consumed by his loved ones' suffering to prevent my mastery of Merlin's staff. I *will* bring you out of the Heartstone, just as I *will* bring about the Eternal Night."

Even from behind the marbled sheath of

Heartstone, Gunmar studied Morgana. She considered this strategy, until the Dark Trollmarket shuddered with an even stronger rumbling. Gunmar's single, incensed eye caught one last glimpse of his son before Bular's body crumbled into a pile of pebbles once more.

The Dark Underlord resisted the acute, feral urge to howl—to let loose a cry of abject suffering. Morgana's silhouette cackled and unstitched itself. Even as she faded, her shrill, sadistic laugh echoed louder in Gunmar's mind than the tremor that had just leveled his son.

CHAPTER 14
FOR THE LOVE OF . . .

Normally, Merlin hated to run. It was just so *ordinary*.

But the wizard had to, if he wanted to keep up with Team Trollhunters. Jim led them through the war zone, slashing at vines with his Sword of Daylight and deflecting scalding geysers with his shield. Toby and Claire followed close behind, using their Warhammer and Shadow Staff to trip up any Troll combatants who interrupted their forward progress. Blinky lobbed the occasional Dwärkstone grenade, not to add to the chaos, but to separate River and Garden Trolls with large craters. And AAARRRGGHH!!! guarded the back of the line, his runes glowing green as he swatted away the boulders, arrows, and spears that had been loosed upon his friends.

"Heads up!" said Jim.

He spied two Garden Trolls overturn a large vat of boiling oil from the oil baths. The pitch ignited on the burning battlefield, forming a wall of fire in front of Jim. Without breaking pace, the Trollhunter mentally summoned his helmet and faceplate and leaped through the flames. He landed unsinged on the other side, then looked back at his teammates. They skidded to a halt in front of the wall of fire and waited for Merlin to do something about the blaze. But the wizard lagged behind them, doubled over and gasping for air. He held up a trembling finger as if to say, *one minute.*

"Oh, for the love of—" Claire said, rolling her eyes. "Jim, go—we'll catch up!"

Jim nodded gratefully and broke off on his own. Claire pointed her Shadow Staff at the wall of flames, her face wrenched with the extreme strain.

"C'mon, baby," she grunted at her staff. "How 'bout one little shadow for Mama Skull?"

Claire doubled down on her effort, and a tiny black hole tore open. But it was big enough. The miniscule vacuum sucked all the oxygen out of the inferno, smothering it. With their path cleared, Claire, Toby, Blinky, and AAARRRGGHH!!! saw the Trollhunter's remote silver form finally reach his destination in the distance.

Jim shoved his way through a sea of River and Garden Trolls. Yet, these soldiers weren't fighting. Each of them held out objects of value—hunks of crystal, purses fat with gemstones, milk crates full of human laser disc collections—all to curry the favor of the busy Troll before them: Ballustra. She stood atop one of her siege engines—a massive cannon on wheels with a long crystal barrel—conducting transaction after transaction. With one hand, Ballustra took the Trolls' offerings. And with the other, she replaced them with her inventions. The lucky Trolls would then run off with their new weapons, eager to test them on any unsuspecting enemies.

Being much smaller than the other bodies around him, Jim snuck his way to the front of the line. He vanished his helmet and held out his hand, just like the rest. The silver fingertips of Jim's gauntlet immediately caught Ballustra's attention. But when she looked into the palm, she didn't see rubies or diamonds. She saw something far more precious. Ballustra gaped at Jim, her widened eyes locking with his.

"Where did you—?" she began, before rethinking it. "Never mind. I . . . I'm far too busy."

Ballustra reached out for more payments, only to notice her customer base had thinned considerably. Behind her, Jim remained rooted, his hand still outstretched. He said, "Take a day off. We insist."

AAARRRGGHH!!!, Blinky, Claire, Toby, and a wheezing Merlin had positioned themselves at the border of Ballustra's weapons bazaar, beating back any prospective clients and buying Jim time—just like he knew they would. The other Garden and River Trolls that had been clustered around him returned to the fray, leaving Jim alone with Ballustra. She took one of the crystalline arrows from her crossbow and held it close to his exposed face.

"Tell your allies to stand down," said Ballustra. "They're bad for business."

"But war's good for business, isn't it?" Jim shot back. "You *wanted* the River and Garden Trolls to stockpile your weapons, didn't you?"

"You could never understand, Trollhunter," Ballustra said, biting into each word. "Just as

Kan—as the one who came before you never could."

"Actually, Kanjigar did understand," said Jim. "It may have happened a little later than either of you would've liked. But being a Trollhunter helped Kanjigar to see things from all sides . . . not just his own."

Ballustra realized that her stance had grown slack. She tightened her grip on the arrow and brought it closer to Jim's jaw. But the Trollhunter didn't flinch.

"And I'm pretty sure I understand now too," Jim continued. "I was so wrapped up in my own grief, I didn't even bother to notice your own. Yesterday, I lost a friend. But today . . . today you found out you lost both a husband *and* a son."

Ballustra screamed and swung her arrow. It missed Jim by a wide margin and snapped against the siege engine beside them. She stood there, motionless, panting, staring at the broken arrow in her hand.

"I'm so sorry for your losses, Ballustra," Jim said softly. "I can't even imagine what you're going through. But I can see you're hurting. Just like I was. Still am, I guess."

He watched Ballustra's wide brow crease with the first admissions of heartbreak, and added, "My friends—my *amazing* friends—they told me everyone needs to handle pain in their own way. And I think yours is to turn that pain outward. To turn it into weapons."

Time slowed to a crawl, and sound became a distant murmur to Ballustra. Slowly, she looked at the war raging around them. The storied feud between the River and Garden tribes had reached a feverish crescendo. Bombs flew. Bodies fell. And both tribes carpeted the cavern with the petrified husks of their slain soldiers—soldiers who still gripped Ballustra's wares.

"How?" she finally asked. "How do I stop the pain?"

"I . . . I don't really know," Jim answered truthfully. "But Kanjigar promised that it will get better. With time . . ."

Ballustra stirred at the mention of her late husband's name, and Jim extended his open hand to her once again. She looked down and, in the Trollhunter's palm, she saw that which was more precious to her than rubies or diamonds. Ballustra saw a ring. Draal's ring. A ring that had been her own, once upon a time.

"Draal loved to fight, but never to start wars," said Jim. "He fought to *end* them."

A single tear trickled from Ballustra's eye as she looked up at the Trollhunter. She took the ring from his hand and reinserted it in her nose. Jim was struck by how much she now resembled Draal.

"I built those," Ballustra said, gesturing to her various weapons on the battlefield. "And I alone know how to disarm them. In my smithy, I have a fail-safe, a—"

A low, otherworldly wail echoed through the ravaged cavern. Claire had to cover hear ears. The squeal sounded like the feedback she, Darci, and Mary would sometimes hear when their microphones got too close to the speakers during band rehearsals—only a million times worse.

"Oh, grumbly Gruesomes," Blinky muttered in dreadful realization.

"What is it?" Toby yelled.

"I just told you!" Blinky yelled back.

Dozens of elongated, faceless creatures stretched into the cavern. Like a flock of carrion birds, they consumed the scraps of petrified Trolls littering the entire battlefield—including the spot in which Jim and his assembled friends now stood. With dawning horror, Blinky pointed his four hands at the pitiless scavengers swirling around them and shouted, "GRUESOMES!"

CHAPTER 15
GIANT WORM FOOD

"What the flip are those?!" Steve Palchuk shrieked.

He ducked behind the much smaller Eli Pepperjack, who adjusted his glasses and squinted at the three creatures burrowing under Barbara's front lawn. Their bioluminescent dorsal blades tilled the earth, while the rest of them remained beneath the ground . . . for now.

"Th-those are the biggest creeps I've ever seen!" Eli stammered.

"Just wait until they grow to their full size," said Strickler. "But why have Gunmar's Nyarlagroths congregated around *this* block in particular . . . ?"

"Whoa, whoa, whoa—back it up, turtleneck!" Steve interrupted. "Did you say 'Gunmar'? As in, that one-eyed weirdo Pepperjoke mooned a couple of weeks ago? Surely you don't mean *that*, Gunmar?"

"Ste-*eve*!" Eli whined. "Ix-nay on the ooning-may in front of the adies-lay!"

Now blushing with embarrassment, Eli turned to Barbara, dropped the Pig Latin, and pleaded, "Please don't tell my mom, Dr. Lake! It wasn't even me who mooned Gunmar! It was Romeo! Well, Romeo's kinda me, but because of the Grit-Shaka, and—"

"You know what? I don't even want to know," Barbara said.

Everyone nearly lost their balance as the house's foundations shuddered under their feet. Strickler steadied himself and said, "I suppose you *were* right all along, Barbara. We do need to leave this house. But we'd never slip past the Nyarlagroths. They may be blind, but they'll feel our footsteps and swallow us whole before we even reach your car in the driveway."

"Follow me," said Barbara as she hurried to the garage.

Outside, the Nyarlagroth's circled like subterranean sharks. But the endless churning stopped when the monstrous trio heard Barbara's car alarm reverberate through the soil. Their eyeless heads broke through the ground, ravenous jaws snapping at the empty sedan.

While the Nyarlagroths were distracted by the alarm, the garage door opened, and Barbara Lake turned a key in the ignition of an altogether different vehicle. She raced out on Jim's Vespa, with Strickler sharing the seat behind her. Steve followed on Jim's borrowed bicycle, towing Eli, who coasted on his Zip Slippers and shouted, "Spectacular!"

Together, they bypassed the Nyarlagroths, which were still confounded by Barbara's car alarm, but they braked hard once they hit the cul-de-sac. Another three eel creatures tunneled around Nana's property, upsetting the flower beds. On the roof, just outside Toby's bedroom window, Barbara spotted Nana, Dictatious under his sunproof cloak, and Chompsky with Sally strapped to his back.

"Scrambling the Nyarlagroths' senses was pure genius, Barbara, but you can't rescue everyone," Strickler said matter-of-factly. "Best to step on the gas and save our own skins."

"Walt!" Barbara protested. "Nana Domzalski has been my neighbor since Jim and Toby were toddlers. I will not leave that woman to be giant worm food!"

Strickler raised his hands in apology and said, "Fine. But we'll need another distraction."

Steve yanked the slingshot from Eli's back pocket, loaded a rock into its elastic band, and fired. The rock smashed into the rear windshield of Nana's own car, setting off its alarm too.

"Steve, you can't keep vandalizing old people's cars!" Eli said. "We're the good guys!"

"You wanted a distraction, didn't you?" Steve replied.

Indeed, Steve's ploy had worked. Nana's alarm drew the attention of these three Nyarlagroths, just as Barbara's alarm had confused the others. But now Barbara, Strickler, and the Creepslayerz heard the honking of a third car horn. The Nuñez family SUV turned a sharp corner and sped down the block, the final three Nyarlagroths trailing it. But the eels stalled once they got in range of the car alarms, paralyzed by the sonic assault.

Ophelia slammed on the brakes, stopping under Nana's roof. Barbara, Strickler, and Steve climbed up the hood and helped Nana, Dictatious, and Chompsky down the rain gutter. As the others worked, Eli peeked in the SUV and saw Enrique and NotEnrique strapped into two baby seats. The little Changeling spit out his baba and said, "What're you starin' at, Dorkstone?"

Above them, Nana's orthopedic shoe slipped on the gutter, but Steve managed to catch her. Nana batted her eyes and said, "Such a strapping young man! Just like my Horace!"

She planted a big, wet smooch on Steve, making him blush and shudder at the same time. He quickly passed Nana on to Strickler, then pawed the old lady kiss off his cheek. Barbara waved them over and said, "The sooner everyone piles in, the sooner we can drive away from these mutated gophers!"

"We'll never escape them."

Everyone turned to Dictatious, who stood on top of the SUV like a very bizarre hood ornament. His six milky eyes could not behold the sunset colors in the sky that so captivated his brother. And yet he saw things all too clearly. Dictatious stared ahead, adding, "Nyarlagroths can smell the stink of the Darklands on any who have traversed that dismal dimension . . . and all that they have touched."

"So *that's* why they've honed in on this neighborhood," said Strickler. "Each of us has either come from the Darklands or knows someone who has."

"Fine, we can't outrun the Nyarla-whatevers," Barbara accepted. "But is there a way to, I don't know, send them back?"

"To the Darklands?" cried Dictatious. "But how?"

Strickler's eyes flared yellow with an idea. Adopting his most professorial posture, he clapped the Creepslayerz' backs and said, "Misters Palchuk and Pepperjack, how would you like to earn a little . . . *extra credit*?"

CHAPTER 16
DUST TO DUST

"And I thought *I* had a big appetite!" said Toby, both impressed and grossed out.

The Gruesomes swarmed the devastated cavern, bingeing on the ruins of war. Their sallow, rubbery faces bore no features, save for the gibbering maws that feasted upon the dead.

Watching the Gruesomes cannibalize the Troll parts triggered a flashback in Jim. He unwillingly recalled his time in the Darklands, when he saw an Antramonstrum do the same thing to a heap of slaughtered Gumm-Gumms.

"It . . . it's horrible," Claire managed to say.

"I disagree," Merlin shared, not that anyone asked him. "True, many Trolls have died here this day. But their deaths make it possible for the

Gruesomes to live. It's a natural balance."

Some of the surviving River and Garden Trolls turned away from each other. They used their weapons to poke at the creatures in morbid curiosity. Despite lacking nostrils, the Gruesomes sniffed the prodding Trolls, whose bodies had become dusted with the pulverized remains of their fallen comrades. Then, without warning, the Gruesomes unhinged their jaws and devoured the living Trolls in exaggerated gulps.

"I take it all back," Merlin said, going pale. "The natural balance is terrible."

Team Trollhunters looked down at their own bodies, similarly coated in dead Troll dust.

"RUN!" Jim yelled.

"*More* running?" Merlin moaned as everyone else took off ahead of him.

All around them, the River and Garden Trolls, once so heatedly entwined in combat, now fled from the Gruesomes and each other. AAARRRGGHH!!! tossed Toby and Claire onto his back, while Blinky sprinted alongside Jim and Ballustra.

"Master Jim, would it not be more advisable to flee in the other direction, rather than *backtrack*

from whence we came?" said Blinky.

"The River and Garden tribes may be beating a retreat right now, Blink," Jim said back. "But we all know they'll go back to feuding once the Gruesomes eat their fill and move on."

"They will war until no Troll is left standing," Ballustra said. "Unless we reach my fail-safe—a kill switch that would sabotage every weapon I've built!"

"Armistice," AAARRRGGHH!!! grumbled in understanding.

Howls—alien and piercing—sounded from behind as they reached the caved-in entrance to Ballustra's workshop. Jim looked back and saw the Gruesomes close in, fluid forms corkscrewing around every obstacle in their path.

"Jim, you guys go on ahead without us," Claire said, hopping off AAARRRGGHH!!!'s back. "We'll buy you some time!"

She aimed her Shadow Staff at a lunging Gruesome, and opened another microscopic black hole. The vortex sucked up the insatiable invertebrate, pulling it apart like so much taffy. AAARRRGGHH!!! grabbed another before it could latch on to him. The normally gentle Troll stuffed the Gruesome's hindquarters into its own mouth, like a snake eating its own tail.

"Oooh, nice ouroboros!" Toby complimented as he smashed a third with his Warhammer.

Jim led Blinky and Ballustra through the debris-clogged tunnel. They reached the smithy, which was a shambles, tools and tables overturned from explosions and looters.

"The kill switch must be here somewhere," Ballustra said, digging through the detritus.

But her hands stopped when they grazed across something else. It was Draal's cold, stone hand. Jim sensed Ballustra's sudden stillness, then saw what she saw. The Trollhunter joined the grieving mother, sharing in her moment of silence.

"I don't mean to be insensitive, but time is short," Blinky said, four hands cupped to his ear so he could listen down the tunnel. "It sounds as if something's slipped past our friends!"

He squinted his six eyes into the passage— right when a Gruesome sprang from the darkness. Blinky had barely ducked before it poured past him and into the workshop. The Gruesome's blank face hissed with interest around Draal.

"Stay away from him!" shouted Jim, sweeping it away with his Sword of Daylight.

Ballustra rose, her posture supremely calm, and said, "No, Trollhunter. Let it pass."

"But Draal's body—" Jim started to say.

"Is mere rock now," said Ballustra. "It will only weigh us down for the rest of *our* days."

As her words struck Jim, Blinky backed toward them. He kept the salivating Gruesome at bay by swinging an odd device he'd just found. It looked like a wand, fitted with teal crystals and a central coil spun of fine wire filaments. Blinky was about to bash the Gruesome with the device when Ballustra snatched it away.

"This isn't a club," she said. "It's my kill switch!"

"The fail-safe?" Jim asked, now roused from his worry.

Ballustra tucked it into the pouch on Blinky's belt, while simultaneously removing something else. As the Gruesome squealed, Ballustra secreted whatever she'd just taken into her son's rigid hand.

"Tell your team to admit the other Gruesomes," she said.

"But your workshop . . . your home . . . ," Jim began.

"I have all I need," said Ballustra, her nose ring fluttering as she exhaled in acceptance.

Seeing the certainty in her eyes, Jim nodded to Blinky. The six-eyed Troll ran down the tunnel, out to the main cavern, and shouted: "My friends, a slight change of plans! Our Trollhunter now wants us to *send in* the Gruesomes for some Gorgus-forsaken reason!"

"I sure hope Jimbo knows what he's doing!" said Toby, using his Warhammer like a croquet mallet to punt a few Gruesomes into the tunnel.

"Me too," said Claire while she and AAARRRGGHH!!! corralled several more.

Merlin stepped aside, permitting the final Gruesome to join the rest of its ilk, and said, "As do I . . ."

Inside the workshop, Jim and Ballustra witnessed Gruesome after Gruesome ooze through the tunnel. Once the last had arrived, Jim stopped swinging his Sword of Daylight. He and Ballustra leaped away from Draal, and the famished Gruesomes descended upon him like some grotesque tsunami. Their greedy mouths latched all over his body—including Draal's hand, which still held the activated Dwärkstone grenades Ballustra had taken from Blinky's pouch.

"Go down swinging, Draal," said Jim.

He ushered Ballustra out of the workshop, then heard a series of controlled detonations behind them. Looking back, Jim saw an immense fireball shoot out of the workshop—and right at him. The Trollhunter pushed Ballustra out of the tunnel and quickly secured his helmet over his head. Buffeted by an intense wave of heat, he somersaulted clear of the incendiary blast. The fireball rocketed toward the cavern's domed ceiling, lighting up the entire battlefield with its white-hot glare.

"Thanks," Jim said through his soot-streaked faceplate as Ballustra helped him to his feet.

Toby, Claire, Blinky, and AAARRRGGHH!!! soon joined them. The Trollhunter's faceplate vanished so Jim could get a good look at his friends—only to find one missing.

"Where's Merlin?" he asked.

A giggle answered Jim's question.

Porgon leered at Team Trollhunters from the

center of the war zone. Dried mud caked his face, reminding Claire of those two masks—one smiling, one frowning—that symbolized comedy and drama. The Trickster Troll's hexing arm manned the controls of Ballustra's siege engine. And in his other hand, he held Merlin captive, the wizard's unconscious body trussed in Garden Troll vines.

Seeing her cannon in enemy hands, Ballustra fished her fail-safe out of Blinky's pouch.

"For Draal. For peace," she said before activating the kill switch.

Jim and his friends smiled, expecting the huge weapon aimed at them to spontaneously collapse or otherwise disappear in a puff of smoke. But nothing happened.

Porgon said, "The joke's on you, Trollhunters! Now get ready for the punch line!"

And with another giggle, the Trickster Troll trained the siege engine on Jim and his friends and opened fire.

Well, that sure is inconvenient, thought Eli as he felt his cellphone vibrate.

He reached into his overstuffed backpack, accidentally elbowing Steve. They crouched together nervously under the bleachers in Arcadia Oaks High School's empty gym.

"Good evening, Eli Pepperjack speaking," the smaller Creepslayer answered into his cell.

"Whattheflipiswrongwithyou?!" Steve whispered urgently, trying to pry away the phone.

"Eli, can you hear me?" Jim shouted from the cell. "I've got a pretty lousy signal here!"

The Creepslayerz felt another, much bigger vibration, this one coming from under them. The bleachers rattled, and the gym ropes swayed from the ceiling like a pair of nooses. Eli dry-swallowed and said, "Uh, Jim, now isn't a good time. . . ."

"Now isn't a good time for me, either!" Jim said over a loud explosion. "Where's Steve?"

Steve snatched Eli's phone, whisper-shouting, "Really, Jim *Flake*?! This can't wait?"

"Steve, don't hang up!" Jim yelled from the other end. "I need pointers from our school's reigning prank champ—you."

Somehow taking this as a compliment, Steve tossed back his hair and grinned—right before a Nyarlagroth head burst through the space between him and Eli. Screaming, the Creepslayerz ran in different directions. The hideous beast didn't know which to follow. So it did as most predators do, and went after the weaker prey.

"Aw, shoot!" said Eli as the Nyarlagroth chased him. "Why do they always go after me?"

With his loaded backpack weighing him down, Eli roller-skated on the varnished gym floor. Steve ran in parallel, still yelling into the phone while also making a beeline for the exit. They both barged through the doors and onto the PE field at the same time, the screeching

Nyarlagroth in hot pursuit. In a panic, Steve tossed the phone back to Eli. Eli bobbled it from hand to hand as the eel creature slithered under his Zip Slippers.

"Whoa-a-a!" Eli squeaked while skating down the serpent's spine.

An unexpected thrill replaced Eli's terror. He wheeled between the Nyarlagroth's dorsal blades and flipped off its tail like it was a half-pipe. As Eli soared, he felt both happy that no students had lingered at school after hours and seen the Nyarlagroth—and sad that this meant no one was around to witness his sick skating moves. Eli stuck the landing behind the enormous eel and cried, "Steve! Steve, did you *see* that?!"

Stunned by Eli's acrobatic prowess, all Steve could do was form his hand into a *C* for Creepslayerz and say, "Eli . . . that was *spectacular*."

The guys performed their secret handshake, then hauled butt as the Nyarlagroth reared around and resumed its hunt.

Now that dusk had settled, Arcadia's sidewalks appeared mostly clear of pedestrians. But the roads were filled with a different sort of traffic. The Nuñez family's SUV fishtailed around the corner of Main Street and Delancy, followed closely by eight nimble Nyarlagroths. Manhole covers popped and fire hydrants burst as the sightless snakes hounded the speeding vehicle. Ophelia took a sharp left, jostling Javier in the passenger seat; NotEnrique, Nana, and Enrique in the back; and Barbara, Strickler, Dictatious, and Chompsky (and Sally) in the trunk.

"Now do you see why I wanted the four-wheel drive?" Javier asked his wife.

Behind them, Barbara glanced out the rear windshield and said, "I really hope Elijah and Stevie are okay on that mission of yours, Walt."

"They'll be fine," Strickler said. "Ophelia, could you please take your next right?"

She pulled hard on the wheel, turning onto a dirt path through the woods. As the SUV bounced on uneven terrain, Nana said, "Oh, I do love a good high-speed chase!"

Checking the rearview mirror, Ophelia saw trees topple behind them as the Nyarlagroths drew nearer. She tried to accelerate, but the pedal was already to the metal. The SUV roared out of the woods, careening directly toward the dry canal.

"Whatever you do, do not stop until I say so," Strickler instructed.

The city councilwoman was normally a responsible driver. But today she followed Strickler's orders and drove over the edge of the canal. The SUV raced down the steep concrete slope, picking up velocity as it went. Reaching the bottom, the undercarriage scraped against the canal floor with a flurry of sparks, and Strickler yelled, "Stop!"

All four tires braked hard, leaving smoking skid marks. The SUV's many passengers filed out through the doors and trunk and looked up. One by one, eight enormous eels crashed headfirst into the canal's retaining wall. The concrete cracked but did not break, and the Nyarlagroth's groans were quickly replaced by cheers.

"¡Sí!" shouted Javier Nuñez.

Even Barbara seemed impressed. She smiled at Strickler and said, "Well played, Walt."

"Well, it was a team effort, although I fear this reprieve is only temporary," he said.

"Yo, turtleneck!" yelled Steve.

He and Eli raced Jim's Vespa down the opposite retaining wall and over to the SUV. They opened Eli's backpack and pulled out several stone rings that glowed a sickly green.

"I see you had no trouble finding the Fetches in my old office," said Strickler.

"That part was easy," panted Eli, handing over the Fetches. "It was the not-getting-eaten-by-a-giant-creeper part that was a little touch-and-go!"

The ninth Nyarlagroth that had been pursuing Steve and Eli erupted to the surface behind them, just as its eight siblings did at the other end of the canal. The eels looked immense in the twilight, their cylindrical bodies thicker than the oaks they'd just uprooted.

"No," Strickler gasped at the colossal creatures. "I hadn't realized they'd grown so quickly! They'll never fit in these Fetches!"

The group's optimism sank and their fear rose as the Nyarlagroths wormed down the canal. And although cataracts occluded Dictatious's eyes, a certain glimmer of insight suddenly shone within them. He snapped four sets of fingers and said, "The Fetches—let me have them!"

Strickler handed over one. The blind Troll ran his fingers along its iridescent surface, muttering, "Yes! I built this one during my exile—hewn from the Darklands' very bedrock!"

Dictatious snapped the Fetch in two, prompting Strickler to cry, "Have you gone mad?"

The Nyarlagroths continued down the concrete retaining walls, their progress slowed by the feel of the unfamiliar, manmade material on which they squirmed. But Dictatious didn't miss a beat. He handed the broken halves to Barbara, then took another Fetch and broke it, too.

"The Fetches are modular in design," he explained. "There's no way to carve a single slab of stone into so intricate a shape. It must be done by fitting together interlocking pieces—"

"Pieces that can be rearranged into new shapes . . . ," said Eli, catching on.

NotEnrique snagged the remaining Fetches and said, "If ya want somethin' broken, leave it to the experts!"

The imp gave the stone rings to Enrique, who gurgled contently while smashing them to bits against the canal floor.

"I'm so . . . proud?" said Ophelia with great confusion.

"Now, we must all rearrange the pieces into one. Hurry!" barked Dictatious.

Doing their best to ignore the putrid stench of the encroaching Nyarlagroths, the ragtag group of neighbors—male and female, young and old, human and otherwise—recombined the components of the nine individual Fetches into a single, oversized ring.

"*Nig omnu sekko!*" Dictatious incanted in Trollspeak.

A great, swirling portal opened within the Über-Fetch. Even from a few feet away, Barbara Lake could feel the chill of the Darklands wafting out from the other side.

"Jim spent two weeks in *there*?" she said, her face blanching.

A Nyarlagroth flicked its tongue at Strickler. But Barbara tackled him out of the way before the tendril lanced through his chest. They tumbled to the ground, arms around each other, and Barbara said, "Who needs protection *now*?"

If Walter Strickler had a witty response, it was drowned out by a burst of static as one juvenile

Nyarlagroth dove into the Über-Fetch, followed by another, and another.

"Neep!" said Chompsky, holding Sally-Go-Back tight.

"He's right—it's working!" Nana seconded.

Like some nightmarish train returning to the land of the dead, the remaining eels siphoned out of the surface world and into the Darklands. When the last tail cleared the threshold, the Über-Fetch collapsed under its own pull and swirled in after the Nyarlagroths.

As the others stared in shock at the spot where the portal used to be, Barbara and Strickler self-consciously pulled apart and avoided each other's gaze. Being exposed to the Darklands, however briefly, shook Barbara to her core. But it also filled her with some small shred of hope. Because if her son could handle the horrors of that place, then Jim could definitely survive whatever he faced now.

CHAPTER 18
NO TAKE-BACKS

There's no way I'm surviving this, Jim thought as a cannonball shot straight at him.

He flicked his wrist, fanning out the shield on his left gauntlet. The enchanted metal of the Daylight Armor absorbed most of the impact. But the blast still sent the Trollhunter tumbling backward into a rut, next to Ballustra.

"I warned you not to leave this trench," she said. "My siege engine never misses."

"It was worth a shot. Literally," Jim replied, his ribs aching.

He braved a peek over the edge of their furrow and saw the siege engine blow more craters into the battlefield. Porgon controlled Ballustra's cannon with his hexing arm, braying madly at the wanton destruction. Jim then saw Merlin, still unconscious and vine-bound beside the trickster.

"At least Blinky and AAARRRGGHH!!! are okay," Jim added, spotting his Troll friends giving six thumbs up from another foxhole fifty yards away. "Any sign of Toby and Claire?"

"Toe-Buh-Ahs and Cla-Uhr have not returned since you dispatched them," Ballustra said in the same stilting tone Draal once used.

Jim looked down and saw his cell at the bottom of the trench, beside Ballustra's kill switch. The outer casings were cracked open, with the fail-safe's fine wires threaded around the phone's internal antenna. Its touchscreen showed only one percent of battery life, but an astonishing eighteen bars of reception.

"Your kill switch may not have stopped that siege engine, but at least it gave us one heck of a signal boost," said Jim, recalling his frantic call with the Creepslayerz. "I know Claire and Tobes will come through. We just need to free Merlin. He's the key to this entire plan."

More shrapnel rained on them as another crystal cannonball struck nearby. Ballustra calculated the distance between their position and the wizard, and said, "Give me your hands."

Jim overcame his trepidation and did as told. Ballustra grabbed his hands and lifted him bodily. She placed Jim's feet atop hers, pressed his back against her chest, and intertwined their fingers. To Jim, it almost felt like he now wore a second set of armor on top of his Daylight suit. Ballustra winked down at him and said, "Draal and I used to play when he was but a babe. We called it 'Rollie Trollie.'"

Jim felt Ballustra's firm legs propel them up and over the trench. As their bodies arced into the ashen air, hers folded into a ball around his. Ballustra encased the Trollhunter in her spiky form, and they hit the ground rolling.

So, this is how it felt for Draal! Jim thought.

Together, Jim and Ballustra spun like a living cannonball. Porgon's eyes bugged as he saw them coming on a collision course. He hexed the siege engine to fire another fusillade. But Ballustra expertly zigged and zagged across the pockmarked battleground, dodging the cannonballs and aiming toward a raised ridge. She and Jim launched themselves off the natural ramp and separated in midair. With their momentum still carrying them forward, Ballustra knocked Porgon into the siege engine, while the Trollhunter sliced the vines off Merlin with his Sword of Daylight.

But a wave of dizziness promptly struck Jim, and he fell onto his rear next to the wizard. Merlin cracked open one eye, then the other.

"You're awake!" Jim said, verging on nausea. "Did Porgon hit you with some kind of sleeping hex?"

"Don't be preposterous," Merlin yawned. "I just needed another nap."

Jim's jaw went slack. Fortunately, Blinky and AAARRRGGHH!!! ran over from their refuge. Blinky dusted off the Daylight Armor and said, "An audacious attack, Master Jim! Worthy of Draal the Deadly himself!"

The siege engine stirred, and Porgon crawled out from underneath its cracked barrel. He reached for one of Ballustra's abandoned crossbows with his glowing hex hand. Giggling anew, Porgon then aimed the weapon at its maker.

"Oh, do be quiet," said Merlin.

Porgon's laughter died. He looked down and felt along his lips, which had been turned to solid, unmoving stone by the wizard.

"Much better," grumbled AAARRRGGHH!!!

"Mmf mmf mmf!" Porgon cried in muted protest.

"Sorry," said Merlin. "No take-backs."

Jim cocked an impressed eyebrow and said, "That was some parlor trick!"

"A little rest goes a long way, Trollhunter." Merlin grinned.

"Jimbo!" Toby's voice called from afar.

Toby and Claire sprinted toward them across the deserted battlefield, the scored landscape picked clean of Troll remains. They looked like they were in a serious hurry.

"Mission accomplished?" asked Jim.

"See for yourself!" Claire answered before pulling herself and Toby to the ground.

A pack of Gruesomes spurted past them and landed around Porgon. Their elastic mouths salivated in hunger at the Trickster Troll's petrified jaw. Porgon strangled out a sound of muffled fear. As the Gruesomes inched closer, he noticed how they had numbers painted on their sides. It was like some absurd joke that Porgon didn't get.

He fired Ballustra's crossbow at the scavengers, skewering the Gruesomes numbered 1, 2, and 4 before he ran out of crystalline arrows. Porgon's panicked eyes scoured the war zone for the last Gruesome—number 3. *Where was Gruesome number 3?!*

Merlin cupped his emerald hands together and blew into them, simulating the squelching howl of a Gruesome. If Porgon could open his stone jaws, he would've let out a high-pitched scream. Instead, the Trickster Troll dropped the spent crossbow and fled the cavern. As he ran, he compulsively looked back with a gripping fear of the entity that would dine upon his mouth—a mouth that would never laugh again. And so Porgon would forever run from the invisible menace of Gruesome number 3.

"There is no Gruesome number 3, is there?" said Merlin, amused. "Most clever."

Jim high-fived Claire and Toby—their hands still caked in the mud used to paint the food-comatose Gruesomes they'd found—and said, "Nope. But I can't take the credit. That prank was pure Palchuk."

Jim's mind drifted back to what Steve had told

him during their brief, hot-wired phone call. Was it only last semester when Steve wanted to get even with Señor Uhl for a failing grade in Spanish? When Steve broke into school one night and snuck three cows into Uhl's classroom—three cows numbered 1, 2, and 4? When Señor Uhl spent the better part of a week scouring the hallways, muttering angrily in Spanish *and* German, searching in vain for a phantom cow number 3? When the tormented teacher dropped to his knees and screamed to the heavens, finally realizing that there really was no cow number 3?

The memory brought a grin to Jim's face. A grin that spread into a smile. And for the first time since Draal died, the Trollhunter laughed.

"Now," said Merlin in satisfaction. "*Now* you are ready to go home."

FILLING THE VOID

Yes, in all his many centuries of life, Kanjigar had known much happiness.

But even those milestones couldn't compare to the transcendent jubilation he now felt as a familiar figure materialized in the Void. Kanjigar the Courageous's spirit glided over to the newcomer and said, "Welcome to the afterlife of Amulet bearers. The warden of warriors. The hall of heroes. Welcome home . . . my son."

Draal the Deadly blinked open his eyes, looking down at—and right through—his transparent body. He opened and closed his hands, seeing how his right arm had somehow regrown in this misted, magical plane.

"F-father?" Draal said, his consternation soon becoming a chuckle. "Father!"

Kanjigar and Draal embraced, their spirits lifting figuratively *and* literally. They twirled together in the weightless space, only pulling apart enough to get a good look at each other.

"But . . . how can this be?" Draal asked, his joy bordering on tears. "Is Mother here too?"

"In a sense," said Kanjigar, tilting his horns to the side.

Draal followed his father's gaze to an orb of light, which flattened and expanded into a scrying window. Through this levitating looking glass, he saw the war-torn cavern, where Ballustra, Jim, and the rest of Team Trollhunters presided over a meeting between the surviving Trolls. He listened eagerly as Ballustra addressed the Garden Troll Elder and the River Troll Ruler.

The two leaders gave each other a long, hard look before joining hands and knocking together their heads three times in a solemn Troll oath. All those who bore witness burst into a cheer of relief and congratulated one another.

"I know we'll be half a world apart," Jim said to Ballustra. "But I hope we stay in touch."

"On this you may count," Ballustra replied.

"Now that my career as a weaponsmith has ended, I thought I might ply my Monger skills in a new trade—communication."

She handed Jim his cell phone, totally repaired and fully charged, to boot.

"Thank you, Trollhunter, for bringing me closer to my son than I ever thought possible," Ballustra added, her nose ring glinting.

"It's the least I could do," Jim said. "I mean, your son helped out *my* mom a lot. I'm just repaying the favor."

Ballustra's broad lips curled into a grin, and she nodded a final farewell. Once Jim rejoined his friends and Merlin, Claire opened a big, fat shadow with her staff and said, "Next stop: Arcadia!"

As Draal's erstwhile teammates shadow-jumped away, he looked expectantly to his father. Reading his son's face as easily now as when he was a boy, Kanjigar beckoned over another scrying portal. This one offered a view inside Claire's house, later that night. Draal looked on with interest as the Nuñez family hosted an intimate ceremony celebrating his own life. Team Trollhunters, their extended families, and a bevy of refugees from Trollmarket crowded into the once-orderly home, drinking glug and trading stories about their fallen friend.

Javier offered food to the assorted Trolls, who all declined when they found out chorizo wasn't a type of sock. Ophelia asked if any of the Trolls were registered to vote. And Nana took pictures of all the revelers. Among her photos was one of Blinky and Dictatious arguing over how to properly teach Troll lore to the Creepslayerz, plus a lovely portrait of the entire Nuñez family—including a surprisingly photo-shy NotEnrique.

Draal was touched by the outpouring of emotion in his honor, but one scene in particular caught his eye. He watched Jim approach Toby in Claire's backyard.

"Tobes, I owe you a *serious* apology," Jim began. "You just were trying to cheer me up when I was down about Draal, and I . . . I . . ."

"Dude," Toby interrupted. "As our late, great pal would say, 'Don't make it weird.'"

Toby held out his arms, and Jim stepped into hug. The sight warmed Draal's heart. Well, whatever passed for a heart in this afterlife. Reminded of his sudden appearance there, Draal said, "Father, I do not mean to seem ungrateful, but how is it that I came to arrive in the Void?"

"I know not, Draal, but I suspect *he* might have an inkling," Kanjigar answered.

Draal peered through the looking glass into Claire's home once more. He saw Merlin, standing alone by the buffet line, munching on a piece of celery. The wizard looked up and winked— seemingly making eye contact with Draal across time and space. Merlin then returned the half-eaten celery stick to the catering platter and walk away.

"What an odd little man," said Draal's spirit.

"Truer words were never spoken, my son," agreed the ghost of Kanjigar. "Though Merlin shall have a crucial part to play in the tribulations ahead."

Father and son turned to a third scrying window, this one focused upon the Dark Trollmarket. There, Gunmar the Gold muttered in Trollspeak while channeling the Staff of Avalon's emerald energies into the base of the Heartstone. The strain of magic against crystal created a wave of arcane feedback, knocking Gunmar to his knees. Queen Usurna ran to his side, only to find a series of runes revealed along the length of the staff.

"'Only human hands may wield,'" she translated. "But how are we to find a human who can speak the Trollish incantation?"

The Gumm-Gumm king punched the floor in rage and said, "Find me an *Impure*. . . ."

"My Trollhunter—my friend, Jim . . . his life's in danger," Draal realized in the Void. "Yet I now find myself unable to come to his defense. I . . . I have failed him, Father. I do not deserve to be with you."

Kanjigar put a consoling hand on Draal's back and said, "You are many things, but a failure is not one of them. How else would you explain your inclusion in this final resting place of Merlin's champions? Draal, you have *more* than earned your seat in the Council of Trollhunters. Not because you held some amulet, but because you held steadfast in your devotion to family and friends. You were as fierce in your loyalty as you were in combat. My son belongs in the Void not because of the way he died, but because of the way he *lived*."

Draal looked up, moved by his father's words. With wide, searching eyes, he returned to the second scrying window. It now revealed Jim and Claire helping Ba-Bru-Ah patch up some cracks left by the Nyarlagroths in Draal's old basement. Witnessing their camaraderie, their obvious love for one another, Draal felt his very soul fill with an inexplicable sense of calm—of peace.

Though the Eternal Night loomed closer than ever, Draal the Deadly knew his Trollhunter would be ready to face a war even greater than the one waged by the River and Garden Trolls. At the very least, Jim Lake Jr. would have one more guardian spirit watching over him from the Void.

"I spent so much of my existence preparing for battle, I never stopped to consider what I'd do once the battle ended," Draal confessed to his father.

Kanjigar held his son and said, "We now have an eternity to figure that out . . . together."

RICHARD ASHLEY HAMILTON

is best known for his storytelling across DreamWorks Animation's How to Train Your Dragon franchise, having written for the Emmy-nominated *DreamWorks Dragons: Race to the Edge* on Netflix and the official DreamWorks Dragons expanded universe bible. In his heart, Richard remains a lifelong comic book fan and has written and developed numerous titles, including *Trollhunters: The Secret History of Trollkind* (with Marc Guggenheim) for Dark Horse Comics and his original series *Scoop* for Insight Editions. Richard lives in Silver Lake, California, with his wife and their two sons.